*The new circuit rider makes Amy feel things
she's never experienced before...*

"Tyler, I..." Her voice fell silent, and she lost herself in
his eyes. The moment was too much for either one of
them, and Tyler pulled her against his huge frame, bending her ever so slightly backward to accommodate his
height.

When his lips touched hers, Amy found herself melting against his broad, muscled chest. Molded there against
him, Amy thought she would die from the flood of passion that filled her. Was this love? she wondered as his
mouth moved against hers.

Tyler pulled away only enough to look deep into Amy's
eyes. Amy suddenly realized that she'd wrapped her arms
around Tyler's neck; the impropriety of romancing the
district's circuit rider made her pull away.

"I'm so sorry." She backed out of his arms and found
herself up against the trunk of the tree. "I didn't know, I,
uh... I didn't mean to do that."

Tyler laughed and pulled Amy back into his arms. "Well
I did," he said and lowered his lips to hers one more time.

JANELLE JAMISON is the pen name for Tracie J. Peterson, a very popular inspirational romance writer and regular columnist for a Christian newspaper in Topeka, Kansas.

Books by Janelle Jamison

HEARTSONG PRESENTS

Don't miss out on any of our super romances. Write to us at the following address for information on our newest releases and club information.

Heartsong Presents Readers' Service
P.O. Box 719
Uhrichsville, OH 44683

Beyond Today

Janelle Jamison

Heartsong Presents

Dedicated to: Bud and Cora, Fred and Casey, Pete and Kay, and all the other alias names they go by; with special thanks for the home they've provided, the love they've poured out and the son they shared with me.

ISBN 1-55748-561-5

BEYOND TODAY

one

On the way home from town, Amy Carmichael closed her eyes and rested her head against the edge of the jostling wagon. She was trying desperately to ignore the animated, non-stop rambling of her twin sister, Angie.

Physically, Angela and Amy Carmichael were identical. Considered too tall by most of their peers, the girls measured at exactly five feet, ten inches. Their stature was the only thing their friends could find to criticize, though, for the twins' perfect features and tiny waists had been the envy of all. Now, at nineteen, with dark hair the color of chestnuts and brown eyes like velvet, the twins were envied more than ever.

On the outside, the twins were a beautiful matched pair, so much alike that they confused even their friends. But on the inside. . .

"You're not listening, Amy," Angie commented with a pout.

"No, I suppose I'm not. I'm really tired, Angie." Amy tried to adjust her sunbonnet for the tenth time. She pulled its shade over her eyes, squinting at the October sun that felt as hot as any summer day. She tucked a strand of hair beneath the bonnet, glad for the air's slight crispness that hinted that colder weather was coming.

"Just look at the dress Alice sent me," Angie whined.

Amy sat up and tried to show some interest. Angie was profoundly proud that their older sister Alice had broken away from the frontier prairie life, to live in a big city back east. Their sister understood Angie's passion for city life and often sent Angie hand-me-downs from her city finery.

Amy, on the other hand, had little or no interest in the clothes Alice sent. She'd rather be in calico or homespun any day. In consideration of Angie's feelings, however, Amy reached out and touched the shiny, pink satin. "It is lovely, Angie. You'll look quite the city girl in this."

"Oh, I know," Angie gushed, "and won't the boys be impressed."

Amy grimaced. "Where in the world will you wear it for them to see?"

"Why the barn raising, of course!" Angie continued to chatter away, while Amy waved to one of the neighbors in the wagon behind theirs.

As they made their way home, Amy looked often over her shoulder at the small parade of wagons behind them. She smiled. The harvest had been a good one this year. The corn, sold today for a record price, combined with August's summer wheat, guaranteed that the residents of Deer Ridge would head into winter fully supplied with not only their home grown foods, but also store bought goods and money in the bank; such security was a rarity indeed.

Things had gone so well in fact, that the twins' parents, Charles and Dora Carmichael, were planning a barn raising to erect a much needed livestock barn.

"What do you think he'll look like?" Angie questioned, continuing to rub the satin against her wind-burned cheek.

"Who?" Amy asked, wondering if she'd missed part of the conversation.

"The circuit rider of course. Think of all the wonderful places he's been. I get goose bumps just imagining all the things he's seen. It must be truly spectacular to travel to new places all the time." Angie sighed dreamily. "Don't you ever think of what it'd be like to live back in the city? Don't you ever want to make plans for the future, Amy?"

Amy smiled. "A future beyond today?"

"Oh bother with that," Angie said in frustration. "I remember Grandma always saying that and I hated it then too. A person has to make plans."

"Why?"

"Just because they do." Angie's lips pressed together. "Besides, you're making plans for the future. You just don't know it. You're already rearranging the house in your head, just to accommodate the barn raising and the circuit rider's stay. Now don't tell me you're not, because I know you, Amy Carmichael."

Amy shrugged her shoulders. Arguing with her twin was pointless, so she said nothing at all.

Angie didn't care. She continued chattering as if the conversation had never taken a negative turn. That was the best thing about Angie, Amy thought as she half-listened to her twin; Angie'd argue her point of view, but she wouldn't run it into the ground by fighting.

"Amy," she said now, leaning forward as if to share a great secret. "I heard Mama say that the circuit rider used to live in Kansas City! Imagine that—Kansas City!"

Amy rolled her eyes. Between the satin dress and the circuit rider, Angie was completely daffy. Amy watched while Angie's fingers slid back and forth over the smooth material; she could tell that Angie's fascination with the gown was reaching the point where she would soon sink into an absorbed and silent contemplation. She would be imagining, Amy knew, what she would look like in the dress, what accessories would compliment it, how she should do her hair when she wore it. Amy smiled and sighed; she welcomed the silence.

While Angie dreamed of the party that would follow the barn raising, Amy, as her sister had predicted, calculated the work that would be involved during the day of labor.

Barn raisings were real celebrations, and the entire community would turn out to help. The plentiful harvest, coupled with the news of the circuit rider, made the best of reasons to celebrate.

Amy hadn't realized how much she missed regular church services, what her father referred to as the "calling of the faithful." Now they would have a regular circuit rider, and even if he only came every three or four weeks, it was better than nothing at all.

The small community of Deer Ridge had often contemplated building a church and hiring a full time minister, but nothing had ever come of the plans, much to Amy's disappointment. She remembered the community meeting to decide which they would build and support first—a church or a school. With the many large families supplying donations of felled logs and other building materials, the school easily won.

Amy sighed as she remembered church services back in Pennsylvania. They'd left the civilized east, though, and moved to the wild prairie of western Kansas when she and Angie had been only seven.

Their older brother Randy had been elated at the prospect of an adventure. At seventeen, Randy saw this as an answer to the future. Pennsylvania farms were hard to come by and most of the land near his parent's home was already being farmed. Randy had known he could continue farming his father's land, but he wanted to make a stake for himself; homesteading in Kansas offered him the best chance.

Twelve year old Alice, though, had been miserable, just as Angie had been. They hadn't wanted to leave Pennsylvania. Alice had cried herself into the vapors and had to be put to bed, while Angie had whined so much that she received the promise of a spanking if she didn't settle down.

But despite the trepidations of two of the Carmichael daughters, the family farm was sold and the remaining possessions loaded into a canvas-covered wagon.

Unlike her sisters, Amy thought the whole thing great fun. She loved to run alongside the wagon on the way to their new promised land and hated being made to ride inside with the weepy Alice and whining Angie.

The memory made Amy feel cramped now as she sat squeezed between the supplies for the barn raising. "Pa?" she called up to the wagon seat in front of her where her father handled the team. "I'd like to stretch for a while. Would you stop so I can jump down?"

"Sure." Charles Carmichael smiled. Amy was so much like him—always moving, eager to be doing rather than watching.

Amy scrambled down, and because of the slowness of the heavily loaded wagons, she was easily able to keep pace on foot. Once again, she twitched her sunbonnet back in place. "Pa?"

"What is it, Amy?"

"I was just wondering if you knew anything about the circuit rider. Is he young or old?"

"Can't rightly say, but the district minister said he'd be on horseback. I can't imagine him being too awful old, if he's going to cover all this territory on horseback," Charles answered thoughtfully. "It'd be a might taxing on an older feller."

"And he'll be there for the barn raising and stay the night at the farm with us?" Amy already knew the answer, but she wanted to check the grapevine information she'd received from her sister.

"Yup. It's all settled and ain't we the lucky ones. New barn and a man of God all in the same day. Ain't we the lucky ones."

"More like blessed than lucky," Amy's mother Dora Carmichael put in from the other side of her husband. "Carmichaels don't hold no account in luck."

Charles laughed. "That's for sure, Ma. We'd never have gotten this far on Carmichael luck." The three of them laughed at this, though no one was really sure why. The Carmichaels had enjoyed a good life with many choice blessings, yet something in her father's words had amused them all.

No one who lived on the prairie ever chalked much of anything up to luck. Out here, surrounded by such a vast expanse of wilderness, human beings seemed to dwindle right down to the size of ants. They needed their belief in a pattern made by God, a design that He could see from up above, to give them strength; the thought of luck and chance spoiled the image. Maybe that's why they'd laughed. Whatever the reason, Amy was grateful for the laughter and the love.

❧

Three weeks later found the farm in a frenzy of preparation for the barn raising. The entire community would turn out to help the Carmichaels put up their new barn, as well as celebrate the harvest and the arrival of the circuit rider.

Dora Carmichael spent hours sweeping the farm house floor. The Carmichaels were one of the few families in the community to have a puncheon floor, and Dora prided herself in keeping the long thin boards shining with a glow that rivaled even the finest city homes. Normally, once a month she would scrub the floor with a splint broom made from a piece of hickory—Dora always declared that this was the only way to "gussy up" the worn wood—but now with the circuit rider due to stay the night in the Carmichael house, Dora worked that broom until her arms ached.

The Carmichael farmhouse was by far the largest in the community. It was made now of logs and stood two stories high, but it hadn't always been so. The soddy house had come first. Amy remembered her disappointment the first time she'd seen their new home. It had been made of grass and mud, and the thought of living in a dirt house made Alice and Angie bawl. Amy didn't care for it any more than her sisters, but she looked past the sod and saw her father's pride.

Charles Carmichael had stood proudly with his hands on his hips, the hot, Kansas sun at his back, and sweat dripping down the side of his face. He was dirtier than Amy had ever seen him, but the promise of the future shown clear in his eyes, and his smile was as wide as the Smokey Hills River itself. He had built his family a house; now it was up to them to make it home.

Right then Amy decided to work extra hard to make each day pleasurable for her parents. And that was when she decided to adopt her grandmother's attitude of one-day-at-time, looking no further than that day for trouble, because tomorrow was sure to have even more time to plan for problems. And now, Amy thought with a smile, what with getting ready for the barn raising, she had plenty of work to keep her from worrying about anything that might come later on.

੩

"Amy!" Her mother's call made Amy hasten to pull up yet another bucket of water from the well.

"Coming, Ma." Amy hurried back to the house, slopping water on herself as she ran. She was careful to leave her boots at the back door, as she entered her mother's freshly scrubbed kitchen.

"Just put the water on the stove and help me put these curtains up." Dora Carmichael motioned Amy towards the stove.

Amy poured the bucket of water into a large cast iron pot and put the bucket outside the door. Wiping her wet hands on her apron, she reached up to help her mother place the red calico curtains at the kitchen window.

"Looks real good, Ma." Amy stepped back to get a better look. "That calico made up real nice for curtains."

"Well, it's not too bad if I do say so myself. Especially considering the fact that this was your sister's dress, just last week."

"Don't tell her and maybe she won't fuss," Amy laughed. Angie fought to have less homemade things in the house and more store bought luxuries.

"I just can't understand that sister of yours. Never could understand Alice either." Dora sighed. "Don't they ever stop to think that somebody had to make those things the store buys and resells?"

Amy laughed and put her arm around her mother's shoulders. "Angie only thinks about which one of her beaus she's going to marry and what big city she'll go live in. I don't imagine she thinks about much more than that."

The late October temperatures were unseasonably warm and the window stood open to let in the steady southerly breeze. The calico caught the wind and fluttered like a flag unfurling. "They sure do look nice, Ma," Amy repeated.

⁊a

The 20th of October found the Carmichaels' homestead overrun with friends and family. Amy and Angie's brother Randy was the first to arrive. His growing family was seated in the bed of the wagon behind him.

Amy helped her nephews, Charlie and Petey, from the wagon bed, before taking her two year old niece, Dolly. Her very expectant sister-in-law Betsey smiled at her gratefully.

"How have you been feeling, Betsey?" Amy questioned as the pregnant woman scooted herself to the back of the wagon.

"I've definitely been better. I think it would have been easier to ride bareback, than to sit another mile in this wagon."

Amy laughed at the rosy-cheeked blond and offered her a hand down, but Randy came and easily lifted Betsey up and out, placing a loving kiss on her forehead before he set her feet on the ground. At the site of her father offering kisses, Dolly reached out her arms, and said, "Me too!"

Everyone laughed, but Randy leaned over and gave Dolly a peck on the cheek. "Now, Lilleth Carmichael, I expect you to mind your manners today."

The little girl cocked her head to one side, as if confused by the use of her Christian name, instead of the nickname her brother had given her. Then four years old, Petey had been unable to pronounce Lilleth, and so he announced that he would call her "Dolly", because she looked just like a baby doll he'd seen in Smith's General Store. From that point on it had been official, and Lilleth became Dolly.

"Come on, Betsey. Ma's already got a comfortable spot picked out for you under the cottonwood tree," Amy said. Taking hold of Betsey's arm she led her to the waiting chair.

The farmyard was soon a riot of people and livestock. Randy and Charles had picket stakes already set up for the horses, and the wagons were used as tables or places to sit when taking a break from building.

Amy was to be in charge of the children, thus freeing the women to quilt, cook and visit. Some of the more ambitious ladies were even known to get into the act of helping with the construction. Why, Cora Peterson sometimes shinnied right up to the roof supports to put in a few well placed nails. She said it kept her young, and at seventy years of youth, nobody was going to argue with her.

As the sun rose above the horizon in a golden, orange glow, the final preparations were taken care of. Tents were quickly erected for the purpose of neighbors spending the night, thus saving them the long trip back to town, only to turn around the next day and return to hear the circuit rider preach at the Carmichael farm.

Tables bowed from the weight of food, and the array of tantalizing, mouth-watering delights was never to be equaled. Amy had to laugh, knowing that the overflowing plenty was not even the main meal but for the purposes of snacking only. Huge cinnamon rolls and fresh baked breads lined the tables, along with jars of preserves and jams of every flavor, as well as a variety of butters, apple, peach, and even plum. Someone had thought to bring several long rolls of smoked sausage, which were quickly cut into slices and eaten between bread, before the first log was in place. All in all, everyone deemed it a great day to build a barn.

two

"The preacher's a'comin! The preacher's a'comin!" The children ran toward the two approaching horses.

The excitement was uncontainable among the Deer Ridge residents, and even Angie stopped flirting with Jack Anderson. Another of her boyfriends, who just happened to be Jack's brother Ed, rode into the farmyard with the biggest man anyone in Deer Ridge had ever laid eyes on.

Amy was out of earshot, and so she missed seeing the circuit rider as his six foot, six inch frame bounded down from his huge Morgan horse. Angie, on the other hand, was ready and waiting.

"This is Pastor Tyler Andrews," Ed Anderson told them. Ed was the town's bank teller and the one person Angie figured had a pretty good chance of getting her out of Deer Ridge.

"Howdy do, Parson," Charles Carmichael said, taking the man's mammoth hand in his own.

The giant man smiled. "Please call me Tyler." His voice was rich and warm. "Pastor and Parson sound much too stuffy for friends." Taking off his hat, he revealed sweat soaked golden curls. Angie thought they were divine.

She batted her thick black lashes while her dark eyes slid appraisingly over Tyler. He dwarfed everyone around him, but his brown eyes were welcoming and friendly.

Without warning, Angie reached out boldly and took Tyler's arm. "You simply must meet my mother, Dora

Carmichael. Oh, and over here is Mrs. Stewart. Her husband owns the bank. And this is Mrs. Taggert—her husband is Doc. He's that man over there in the dark coat." Tyler had to laugh as the tall, willowy girl fairly pulled him through the mass of people, completely ignoring Ed Anderson.

If any one in Deer Ridge was surprised by Angie's outburst, no one said a thing. Angie was always livening up things, and today wasn't going to be any different. She had a way about her that endeared her to people about as quickly as she annoyed them. Angie, though, never had any hard feelings; she was simply being Angie, and most people understood that.

Only a handful of people missed getting introduced to the massive preacher by Angie. Most of them were under the age of ten, though, and the only adult not yet privileged to make Tyler's acquaintance was Amy.

Amy had taken the children to play hide and seek and Red Rover in the orchard. She loved the children best. They were demanding, but their wants were simple. They continually asked for drinks and help to the outhouse, but Amy found them easier to be with than the adults. She could simply play with them all morning, and they accepted her just as she was. At the noon meal, the weary and worn children would join their folks and be ready to nap in the afternoon.

"Watch me, Amy! I'm gonna jump out of this tree," eight year old Charlie called to his aunt.

"If you break your leg, don't come crying about it afterwards," Amy called over her shoulder as she hoisted Dolly to her other hip. She was glad she'd chosen to wear her older blue gingham for playing with the children, since Dolly was taking turns chewing first on the collar of the dress and then the sleeve.

"Poor baby," Amy said as she smoothed Dolly's downy brown hair back into place. "Are you getting new teeth? I bet Grammy has some hard biscuits for you to chew on. We'll just see if she doesn't."

Amy put two of the older girls in charge of watching over the others and went in search of a teething biscuit for Dolly. As she rounded the corner of the Carmichaels' two-story log home, Amy could see that the barn was already sporting a frame on three sides. She glanced around, wondering if the new minister had arrived. Spying her mother, Amy made her way to inquire about the preacher and the biscuit.

"Dolly needs a teething biscuit, Ma," Amy said, trying to pull her collar out of her niece's mouth. "Those back molars of hers are causing her fits."

"There's a whole batch of hard biscuits on the table in the house," Dora answered and reached up for her granddaughter. Dolly would have none of it, however, and turned to bury her face in Amy's hair.

"You ought to tie your hair back, Amy," Dora suggested. "She has your hair a mess."

"I tried putting it back three times," Amy answered. "It keeps coming free, mostly because of a little boy named Petey, who thinks it's fun to snatch my ribbon." Amy laughed. Betsey and Dora laughed too.

Amy turned to go to the house when she remembered the circuit rider and turned back. "Is he here yet, Ma?"

"Who?" Dora asked, wondering if her daughter was finally taking an interest in one of the community's eligible men.

"The circuit rider, of course. Who else did you think I was talking about?"

"Oh, no one in particular." Her mother smiled. "I was just hoping, that's all."

"Now, Ma. Don't get started on me and husband hunting. I'll know when the right man comes along. He just hasn't come along yet. So is the preacher here or not?"

"Sure is. See that spot of gold on top of the east edge of the barn frame?"

Amy craned her neck to see the man her mother was pointing out. She could barely see him, but he was there and she felt satisfied just knowing it.

"I'm sure glad he made it. It's going to be fun having a preacher and regular church services again."

"We haven't done so bad with the home services," Dora said, supporting her husband's perseverance in holding some type of Sabbath service for his children and grandchildren.

"Of course not, Ma. I just think it will be nice to get together with the others. Is he nice? What's he look like? I can't really see him too well from here." Amy strained to get a better look without being too obvious.

"Well," her mother answered, "I must say your sister was certainly taken with him. Angie latched onto him first thing, so you'd best ask her if you want to know what he's like. I just barely said hello, before Angie was dragging him off again." Dora laughed and added, "About the one thing I could tell about him is that he's a big man. Taller than your pa and shoulders broad as bull."

"That's for sure." Betsey struggled to get into a more comfortable position.

Amy decided not to seek out the new preacher. After all, if Angie had already set her cap on him, what chance would the poor man have of freeing himself up to meet the likes of Amy?

I don't need to meet him now, Amy decided, going back to tend the children. I'll get to hear him preach tomorrow and maybe even tonight. Let Angie make a fool out of herself. It seems to give her such pleasure.

Amy was enjoying the children so much, she was surprised when someone rang the dinner bell.

"You children run on now and find your folks," she said. "It's time to eat—and I heard tell somebody brought cherry cobbler for dessert." She steered the children in the direction of the lunch tables.

She managed to deposit Dolly into Dora's arms with only a few complaining whimpers from Dolly, and then she went to make sure the other children made it back to their mothers. She glanced around again for a glimpse of the preacher, but he was seated among a huge group of people and she couldn't get a good look at him. She would just have to wait to satisfy her curiosity.

❧

"So that would make you thirty-one years old," Angie said, after mentally calculating the figures she'd just heard Tyler recite.

"That's right, Angie." Tyler grinned. He liked this young woman, so lively and vibrant. She seemed to pull everyone around her into an atmosphere of celebration. "I've been riding the circuit for seven years, with most of my time spent in Missouri. My folks live outside of Kansas City."

"Kansas City!" Angie squealed. "Oh, do tell me what Kansas City is like. I want so much to go there. Have you been to any other big cities? I want to hear about them too!" Angie rambled on, giving Tyler no time to answer.

But before the meal was finished, Angie had managed to learn a great deal about life in Kansas City. She also knew that Tyler Andrews had become a minister after losing his bride of several months to an influenza epidemic.

Stuffed from the heaps of food ladled onto his plate, Tyler excused himself to clean up. Meanwhile, Ed and Jack Anderson had taken as much ignoring as they could tolerate from Angie, and as soon as Tyler got to his feet, they came to reclaim her.

Tyler listened to Angie fuss over the two men and laughed to himself. He shook his head in wonderment, nearly running over Charles Carmichael.

"Pastor Tyler," Charles said, unable to bring himself to use only the man's first name. "I hope you're finding everything you need. The conveniences are behind the house, although I'm sure you could've figure that one out. Feel free to walk around." Charles patted his full belly. "I think I'll take a little nap while the others rest."

"Thank you, Mister Carmichael," Tyler said.

"No, no," Charles protested, "just call me Charles. Everybody else does."

"Only if you'll call me Tyler."

Charles laughed and stuck out his right hand. "It's a deal, Tyler. Although never in my life have I called a man of God by his first name."

"Then it's about time." Tyler shook the man's hand vigorously. "Formalities hold little account with me. We're all one family, after all."

"That we are. That we are," Charles agreed and went off in search of a place to rest. He was going to like this new preacher, he could tell already.

❧

Amy placed the two full buckets of water on either end of the yoke. Careful to avoid spilling any of the precious liquid, she hoisted the yoke to her shoulders. She carried the water to a huge caldron, normally used for laundry and soap making, and dumped it in. After several trips to the well, she lit the kindling and logs beneath the pot so that the water would heat for washing the dishes.

Satisfied that the fire was well lit, she went back to hauling water. She hummed to herself, enjoying the temporary quiet in the aftermath of lunch. The final two buckets hoisted at last to her shoulders, she was startled to find the weight suddenly lifted. She whirled around.

Her mouth fell open as she stared up at Tyler Andrews' giant form. After several seconds, she stammered, "I, I, ah—" She couldn't think of anything to say.

Tyler grinned. "You amaze me, Angie. I wouldn't have thought a little lady like you could've raised this thing, much less carry it very far. How in the world did you manage to give your beaus the slip?" He chuckled, amused by the stunned expression on the face of the woman he thought was Angie.

Amy felt her legs start to shake. What in the world was wrong with her? She hoped she wasn't coming down with a spell of ague, or malaria, as some of the city doctors referred to it. It ran rampant at times, and while Amy and Angie had been lucky to avoid it, Amy knew her mother suffered severe bouts of it.

She struggled to find something to say and finally blurted out the only thing that came to mind. "You must be the circuit rider. I'm glad you decided to come to Deer Ridge."

Tyler looked at her strangely for a moment. What kind of game was Angie playing now? She'd nearly broken his arm dragging him from person to person this morning, and then at lunch she flirted with him unmercifully. Now, she acted as though she'd never met him.

Amy felt her heart pounding louder and faster, until she was certain Tyler could hear it from where he stood. She put her hand to her breast as if to still the racing beat. Tyler Andrews was as handsome as any man she had ever met.

When Tyler just watched her, his brows knit, Amy suddenly realized that he was confused. Apparently, though not surprisingly, Angie hadn't told him she had a twin sister. Amy took a deep breath. "I'm sorry, you must think my manners are atrocious. I'm Amy Carmichael, Angie's twin sister."

A broad smile crossed Tyler's worried face. "That's a relief. I thought for moment you were touched in the head. You know, too much sun."

Amy smiled. "No, just not as forward as my sister. Sorry if we confused you. We're really not up to mischief." She heard her own words, and she thought her voice sounded normal enough, despite the alien feelings inside her body and the clutter of confusion in her mind. "Well," she added with a grin, "at least *I'm* not up to mischief. Once you get to know us, you'll be able to tell us apart. We may look alike, but that's about it."

Tyler laughed out loud. "So there are two of you—and I'll eat my hat if you aren't identical."

"We are that, Pastor," Amy agreed and added, "in a physical sense. We do have our differences, though, believe me."

"I can see that too."

Tyler had forgotten about the weight he still held, but Amy noticed the water and motioned for Tyler to follow her. "You'll burn your muscles out good, standing there like that, Pastor," she said. She wondered whether she should take one of the buckets and ease his burden.

"Just lead the way," he answered, "and please don't call me pastor. I've just worked through that with your pa and finally he's calling me Tyler. I'd like it if you'd call me that too." He followed Amy to the caldron.

She took the pails off the yoke hooks and emptied them into the caldron before answering. "All right, Tyler." She smiled a little, tasting the name for the first time. "And you call me Amy."

Tyler placed the yoke on the ground and extended his hand. "It's a deal."

Amy held out her hand, and Tyler took hold of her small tanned arm with his left hand, as his right hand grasped her fingers. The touch of his warm hands made her shiver. "There's a chill to the air, don't you think?" she said, despite the warm sun that beat down on their heads. She thought she saw a glint of amusement in Tyler's eyes.

What in the world was wrong with her?

three

Despite the jittery feeling that ran along her nerves, Amy found herself comfortable in the company of Tyler Andrews. She showed him around the farm, pointing out things she loved the most.

"There's a path down past the old barn that leads to our orchards," she told him, guiding him back to the construction site of the new barn. "But I can show you later." She noticed that a few of the men were already back at work, and while she was enjoying her time with Tyler, he was probably anxious to get back to the company of men.

In reality, nothing could have been further from Tyler's mind. He was delighted at his good fortune and Amy's company. He'd ridden the circuit for over seven years, always embracing each new community, always enjoying his service to God. But in the back of his mind he had always had the desire to settle down. That desire had made Tyler carefully consider each and every community that he pastored—as a possible home.

Now, as he watched Amy Carmichael speak in her soft, quiet way about the life she loved here on the plains, Tyler began to think he might see the possibility of a lifetime partner—and maybe even a home.

Amy brushed back a loose strand of brown hair and took her red hair ribbon out of her apron pocket. "I tried three times to retie my hair—and each time one of the ornery boys I was caring for this morning pulled it from me and left my hair disheveled. I do apologize for being so unkept." Amy tied the ribbon in place. "Now that the children are napping, I should be safe."

Tyler chuckled, and Amy was surprised to see a strange look of amusement spread across his face. His laughing brown eyes caught the sunshine and reflected flecks of amber in their warmth. There were tiny creases at the corners, betraying his love of laughter.

What manner of man was this preacher? So full of life and laughter. So comfortable and happy to share the small details of life on the farm. Amy smoothed down the edges of her dress collar, now hopelessly wrinkled from Dolly's chewing; she didn't even feel the hand that reached up and pulled loose her hair ribbon.

As the chestnut bulk fell around her face, Amy gave a gasp of surprise. She looked up to see a mocking grin and arched eyebrows, as Tyler dangled her ribbon high above her head.

"Boys will be boys no matter the age, Miss Amy," Tyler said and then put the ribbon in his shirt pocket. Amy started to protest, but Tyler had already moved away to retrieve a hammer. She stared after him, long after he'd climbed the ladder to help her father.

"Better shut your mouth, Amy, or you'll catch flies in it," Angie teased. "Isn't he wonderful!" It was an exclamation, not a question, and Angie fairly beamed as she continued. "He spent lunch with me and told me all about his life. Do you know, his parents still live near Kansas City and they go to the opera and the symphony. Can you imagine it, Amy?"

"No, I truly can't," Amy admitted. The things that attracted her twin held little interest for Amy, and while she hated to hurt her sister's feelings, she couldn't lie.

"If I were to marry that man," Angie continued, "I could

probably live with his parents in Kansas City, while he rode the circuit. Wouldn't that be a dream? Everything in the world at your fingertips!"

"For pity's sake, Angie. The man just arrived in Deer Ridge, and already you're acting as though he's proposed." Amy didn't want to admit the twinge of disappointment she was feeling. Her sister was used to getting her own way when it came to men. Most of them simply fell at her feet whenever she batted her eyes, and now Angie was contemplating the new minister as if he were a prized hog at the local fair. Amy shrugged her shoulders.

"Things move pretty fast among frontier folk," Angie mused with a coy smile. "But, I think I would like to get to know this Tyler Andrews better. I'm going to see to it that he dances at least half the dances with me tonight. I'll bet I can have him proposing before the night is over."

"Angie!" Amy gasped. "You don't even know this man. You surely don't love him, so how can you even think of trying to snag him into marriage?"

"I can love anybody, dear sister. In fact, love is the easy part. I haven't met a man yet that didn't make me feel happy and loved."

"What about the man?" Amy asked and noticed the smile leave Angie's face. "Don't they deserve to be loved by their wives?"

"Well, don't get vulgar about it." Angie feigned a shocked expression. She hated it when Amy revealed a flaw in her ideals, and now she tried to distract her twin by deliberately misunderstanding. "Of course, whatever is expected of a wife would come along with the marriage. I'm sure it can't be too unpleasant."

"You know very well I'm not talking about that," Amy said with a blush. "I'm talking about caring and supporting. That's the kind of loving I'm talking about."

Angie tossed her precisely placed curls. Unlike her twin, she had little trouble keeping her hair pinned, despite the number of suitors that followed her around the farm. "You are such a bother, Amy. I don't want to argue with you, so let's just drop it for the time. I like Tyler, and he likes me. If something more comes about tonight, then it must be meant to be."

With that, Angie bounced off in the direction of the newly arrived Nathan Gallagher. Nathan was Deer Ridge's only lawyer and the third of Angie's more serious boyfriends. Amy shook her head and sighed. Sometimes her sister could be infuriating.

ᴥ

By nightfall the barn was completed, with the exception of some indoor work, and it was as fine a structure as any farmer could ever hope for. Its completion signaled time for supper and everyone knew what would follow that—the dance!

Amy was busy with kitchen work, but she found her thoughts still caught by Tyler. She couldn't help but remember the way his eyes seemed to laugh even before his face cracked a smile. She had already memorized each feature of his handsome face, she realized, and she nearly found herself tracing its lines in the potatoes she was mashing before the clatter of pans behind her brought her back to reality.

She looked around her to see if anyone had seen how silly she was acting, but the bustling group of older women seemed to scarcely notice her presence. Most of the other women Amy's age were outside, enjoying the company of the young men. Through the open window, Amy could hear Angie's exuberant laughter. No doubt she had cornered Tyler again and was working him into her snare.

Amy threw down the potato masher. Why did Angie have to be like that? Trying to ignore the sound of her sister's joy, Amy took the large bowl of potatoes to the table and fled to the safety of her room.

After an hour or more had passed, Amy rejoined the festive crowd. She had changed her grass-stained dress and now wore a soft muslin gown that had been dyed a shade of yellow. The dye was made from golden rod plants, and the color was called nankeen. The gown was simple, with gathers at the waist and a scoop-necked bodice that had been trimmed with handmade tatting. The bodice was a bit snug, as the dress had been made nearly three years earlier, and it accentuated Amy's well-rounded figure and tiny waist.

She had pulled back her hair at the sides and pinned it into a loose bun at the back of her head. Tiny wisps fell stubbornly loose, framing her heart-shaped face, but Amy felt satisfied with her appearance. She shouldn't let Angie's zeal for life annoy her—and she certainly shouldn't let her irritation make her miss the fun of the evening.

Amy stepped into the yard just as the fiddles began tuning up for the dance. Her father had hung several lanterns from poles and trees, and their light cast a hazy glow over the party. The light was so soft, so muted, that Amy felt as though she were in a dream.

She couldn't help but hear Angie's vivacious voice, though. Her twin stood with several girls her own age, telling them about the pink satin she wore. Amy sighed and turned toward the dessert table to help the older women cut pies and cakes.

"Amy!" a voice called out from the sea of people.

Amy was surprised to see Jacob Anderson, younger

brother of Ed and Jack, pushing his way toward her through the crowd.

"Hello, Jacob." Amy smiled. "I didn't know you'd be here tonight. I thought you were still in Hays."

"I wouldn't have missed a chance to dance with you. My, don't you look pretty tonight. How come you won't marry me? We could run off to find our fortune in gold. You know they're pulling nuggets as big as sows out of the Rockies. We could have it all, Amy." Jacob took hold of Amy's elbow. "Come over here where it's quieter and talk with me a spell."

"Oh, Jacob," Amy sighed. "I have a great deal of work to do. Ma counts on me to help out, seeing's how Angie's always so preoccupied." She allowed Jacob to lead her to the back of his family's wagon and accepted his hands on her waist as he lifted her to sit on the edge of the wagon bed. "I can't stay long."

Jacob stood in front of her, his boyish face illuminated by the glow of a lantern that had been mounted on the wagon. "You know how I feel about you, Amy." He took hold of her hands. "I can't stand not being around you and when you're not around, you're all I can think about."

Amy shook her head. Poor Jacob. He wasn't at all interesting to her. He was only a year older than her and so immature with his wild dreams of gold in the Rockies. "How you do go on, Jacob Anderson. How come you aren't taking after Angie, like your brothers?" Amy smiled, hoping to lessen the seriousness of Jacob's face.

He smiled sheepishly, not wanting to admit that he *had* been interested in Angie, but his brothers had threatened to skin him alive if he so much as dared to speak with her. "Don't you think your sister has enough beaus?" he said instead. Amy was every bit as pretty as her sister and she was always kindhearted, listening to his gold rush stories. That made up for a lot, Jacob reasoned.

Amy pulled her hands gently from his. "Jacob," she began, "you know I'm not interested in being courted by you. Why do you keep after me like this?"

Jacob pushed a hand through his blond hair and shrugged his shoulders. "I keep thinking it can't hurt to try. Sooner or later you're bound to come to your senses. Why you're already older than most of the unmarried girls in the county." He grimaced as he realized what he'd said. "I'm sorry, I didn't mean it like it sounded."

Amy laughed and pushed herself off the wagon to stand eye to eye with her suitor. "I know you didn't, Jacob. Don't worry, I'm not Angie and I couldn't care a fig how old I am. I won't marry anyone until I'm in love and know that it's the man God wants me to marry."

Amy left Jacob to contemplate her words and joined her mother at the food table. An array of pies, cakes, cookies and fruit breads lined the long wooden planked table. Amy noticed that here and there someone had placed a cobbler or custard dish, and someone had even gone to the trouble of making a tray of fruit tarts.

"Did I see you with the youngest Anderson boy?" Dora was ever hopeful that Amy would find someone who interested her.

"Yes, Jacob proposed again, in a round about way." Amy laughed. "And, I told him no, in a most definite way."

"One of these days, girl, you're going to have to settle down with someone." Dora reached out to caress her daughter's cheek. "But until you do I'm mighty glad to have you here with me. You're a blessing child, both to me and to your pa."

"I could never doubt that for a minute!" The masculine

voice belonged to Tyler Andrews, and Amy felt her face grow hot with embarrassment.

"I've been looking all over for you," Tyler said with a grin, amused that Amy was so self-conscious, while Angie had boldly flirted with him through a half a dozen reels already. "Come share a dance with me and let me see if twins dance differently from one another."

Amy laughed. "I don't dance nearly as well as Angie. In fact, I quite often avoid the activity if at all possible." Her heart pounded in an unfamiliar way, and she noticed her mouth felt suddenly dry.

Tyler wouldn't be put off. He surprised both Dora and Amy by coming around the table to take Amy's hand. "I won't take no for an answer. Now, if you'll excuse us, Mrs. Carmichael, I intend to waltz with your daughter."

Dora Carmichael nodded and smiled as Tyler fairly dragged Amy toward the other dancers. Amy flashed a look over her shoulder at her mother. Dora shrugged in amusement at the stunned expression on her daughter's face.

"Maybe," thought Dora aloud, "just maybe he's the one." The thought gave her a great deal to contemplate as she watched the new circuit rider take her daughter into his arms.

Amy stiffened at the touch of Tyler's hands on her waist. She felt her hands go clammy and wished she'd remembered to bring her handkerchief with her. She was glad for Tyler's towering height, because usually she had no choice but to look directly into the eyes of her dance partner. With Tyler, however, she was granted the privacy of his chest.

"Relax, you'll do just fine," Tyler whispered into her ear.

But instead of relaxing, Amy felt a shiver run up her spine. Her stomach did a flip, and she felt weak in the knees. "I don't think I can do this," she murmured beneath her breath.

"Of course you can," Tyler said with knowing authority. "Look at me, Amy."

Amy's head snapped up at the command. Tyler's face was only inches from hers, and the look he gave her seemed to pierce her heart. She'd seen looks like this before, but usually they were intended for her sister.

She swallowed hard and unknowingly tightened her grip on Tyler's hand, as she stepped on his toe. She frowned. "I told you I wasn't any good at this."

Tyler laughed and whirled her into the flow of the other waltzers. "You dance perfectly well, Miss Carmichael. I fear it's my inept skills that caused your misplaced step."

"How gallant of you, sir," Amy said, playing the game.

"My pleasure, ma'am," Tyler teased, and Amy found herself relaxing almost against her will.

When the dance ended, Tyler suggested a walk. "You did promise to show me the orchards."

"I did?" Amy tried to remember. "Oh well, come along then."

Tyler took hold of her arm and allowed her to lead. As they passed from the warm glow of the lighted farmyard into the stark brilliance of the moon's light, Amy felt her breath quicken. She chided herself for being so childish. Next thing you know, she thought, I'll be swooning!

Tyler's large, warm hand securely held her arm to keep her from stumbling. He had no way of knowing, of course, that Amy knew this land as well as her own bedroom. He was being chivalrous, as she'd noticed him to be with everyone. Tyler Andrews, she told herself, was simply a gentleman; the caring way he treated her meant nothing special.

Familiar laughter rang out, and Amy and Tyler saw a very busy Angie talking non-stop to a group of four or five men. She was flitting about inside a ring of suitors, as she made promises for upcoming dances.

"That sister of yours is something else," Tyler commented. Amy's response stuck in her throat. She'd always wished she could be more like Angie, and now even Tyler seemed to be as captivated with her twin as most men were. But before she could reply, Tyler continued. "You two are so different. Such a contrast of nature. I thought twins were supposed to be alike."

Amy giggled. The sound touched Tyler's heart with the memory of another tenderhearted woman. A young bride who'd only lived as his wife for a few months before losing her life to influenza.

Seeing Tyler's frown, Amy's laughter died. Her worried look made Tyler say, "I'm sorry. For a moment you reminded me of my wife."

"Your wife!" Amy nearly shouted the words. "I didn't know you were married." She was gripped with guilt for the thoughts she'd been having. Thoughts about how nice it would be to be married to Tyler Andrews. Now she'd coveted another woman's husband.

"I *was* married." Tyler put Amy's racing thoughts to an abrupt halt. "She died over ten years ago. We'd only been married four months when she caught influenza and died."

"I'm sorry." Amy truly meant the words. She'd seen a great deal of death here on the stark, lonely plains of Kansas.

Tyler smiled the sad sort of smile Amy knew people to get when remembering something bittersweet. "Don't be.

She was a frail thing and she was ready to meet God. I've learned not to mourn, but to rejoice because I know she's happy and safe. It was her fondest desire that I not wallow in self-pity and mourning. She even made me promise to remarry."

"I see."

"Losing her made me realize the void in my life. It was then that I decided to become a minister. Circuit riding just seemed to come as a natural way for me, what with the fact that I wasn't tied to one spot. It's been a good life, but I can see the time coming when I'll be ready to settle down to one church and one town." Tyler didn't add the part of his heart that said "and one woman."

"It would be wonderful if you could settle in Deer Ridge," Amy said, not thinking of how her words might seem to Tyler.

"I was just thinking that myself." Tyler smiled at Amy's blunt honesty. "What about you, Amy? Do you have any plans for the future?"

Amy laughed, the sound like music in the night. "You mean beyond today?"

Tyler felt his heart skip a beat as Amy leaned back against the trunk of an apple tree. Her face was lit by the white glow of the moon, and Tyler decided he'd never known a more beautiful woman in all his life.

"That was the general idea," Tyler whispered in a husky tone that was barely audible.

Amy smiled up at Tyler, knowing he didn't understand the Carmichaels' family joke. "I've learned to take it a day at a time. There's too much that's unpredictable in life. My grandmother used to tell me 'Never make plans beyond today!'" Her voice was soft, almost hypnotic, and when she fell silent, Tyler stood completely still, captivated by the moment and the feelings he had inside.

The night was unseasonably warm and the sweet scent of apples still clung to the ground and air around them. Amy couldn't understand why her chest felt tight every time she tried to breath deep. Or why, when she looked at Tyler looking at her the way he was just now, she felt moved to throw herself into his arms. What kind of thought was that for a good, Christian girl?

Used to speaking her mind, Amy suddenly found herself blurting out a confession. "I don't understand what's happening to me. I feel so different. Ever since you appeared at the well, I just feel so funny inside."

Tyler refrained from smiling at this sudden outburst. He was amused to find a woman so innocent and unaware. Surely she must feel the same way he did. After ten years of loneliness, Tyler felt a spark of hope.

Amy frowned as she contemplated her emotions, and Tyler couldn't help but reach out and run a finger along the tight line of her jaw. At his touch, she relaxed. His fingers were warm, and she stood very still, hoping he would not take his hand away.

"Tyler, I..." Her voice fell silent, and she lost herself in his eyes. The moment was too much for either one of them, and Tyler pulled her against his huge frame, bending her ever so slightly backward to accommodate his height.

When his lips touched hers, Amy found herself melting against his broad, muscled chest. Molded there against him, Amy thought she would die from the flood of passion that filled her. Was this love? she wondered as his mouth moved against hers.

Tyler pulled away only enough to look deep into Amy's eyes. Amy suddenly realized that she'd wrapped her arms around Tyler's neck; the impropriety of romancing the district's circuit rider made her pull away.

"I'm so sorry." She backed out of his arms and found herself up against the trunk of the tree. "I didn't know, I, uh. . . I didn't mean to do that."

Tyler laughed and pulled Amy back into his arms. "Well I did," he said and lowered his lips to hers one more time.

four

Sunday morning dawned bright and clear, and the temperature remained warm. Friends from far and wide crawled out from tents, where they had slept on pallets on the ground, and lifted their faces to the sunlight. As the sun rose higher over the brown and gold corn shocks, the shadowy fingers of night disappeared.

Amy watched from her bedroom window. She'd had to spend the night with her sister, because Angie's room had been taken by several of the elderly women in the community, and Amy had had to endure Angie's account of Tyler's life until the wee hours of the morning. She couldn't explain to her twin that Tyler had kissed her, nor could she explain the feelings he had stirred inside her heart.

The fact was, Amy didn't know what to say or think. After all, Tyler Andrews was the new minister, and Amy was nothing more than one of his flock. Or was she?

When Amy finally came downstairs, she could tell by the way people were gathering up their breakfast dishes that the hour was late. Angie had long since departed, anxious to find Tyler and see how he'd fared the night before. Amy was glad she'd chosen to linger upstairs. She felt apprehensive, almost fearful of facing Tyler. What must he think of her after she had wantonly allowed him to kiss her, and not once but twice?

Amy didn't think she could sit in the congregation with family and friends, listening to Tyler Andrews preach, while all the while she was thinking of his kiss. Somehow, she must have led him on; after all, he was a man of God, and surely he had better self-control than she did. Tyler would have no way of knowing how grieved she was by her actions the night before, and Amy longed to apologize.

Amy purposefully avoided the busy kitchen and chose instead the quietness of the back sitting room. "Dear God," she prayed silently, "I don't understand what happened last night and I don't understand the way I feel. I'm truly humiliated at the way I acted and I ask You to forgive me. I asked You long ago to send a strong Christian man into my life, a husband I could love for a lifetime. And," she felt tears form in her eyes, "if Tyler Andrews is the man You have in mind—please show me. I don't mean to be a naive and foolish child, Lord—but like Pa sometimes says, 'I need a good strong sign—one I can't miss.' Please God, please don't let me feel this way towards Tyler if he's not the one. Amen."

Someone began ringing the dinner bell, signaling the time to gather for the services. Amy made her way out the back door of the house and around to where the residents of Deer Ridge were congregating.

She spied Tyler in the crowd, shaking hands and sharing conversation with just about everyone. She also noticed Angie standing to one side of him, her eyes eating up the sight of him in his Sunday best. Amy could almost hear Angie's thoughts as she eyed the cut of his stylish black suit. The string tie he wore at the neck was secured with a tiny silver cross, and beneath the creased edge of his pant legs, his black boots were polished to a bright shine. All in all, the massive man was a fine sight.

Amy tried to slip past Tyler and Angie without having

to speak, but Angie didn't let her. "I saved you a seat, sleepy head," Angie said, taking hold of Amy's arm.

Tyler turned to Amy. Her long brown hair was neatly pinned up, and the wispy strands that fell in ringlets worked with the high necked collar of her blouse to form a frame for her face. He looked at her for several moments before she allowed herself to meet his eyes.

"I thought you'd sleep right through breakfast!" Angie said. "And you tossed and turned so much last night, I thought I was going to have to kick you out of bed to get any sleep."

Amy turned crimson as she caught sight of Tyler's grin. She wanted to run to the safety of the house, but Angie's grip on her arm was firm, and her twin was already rambling on. "I never knew you to get so worked up over a get-together. I swear you mumbled all night long and fairly thrashed me to death."

Amy could no longer stand it. She turned to Angie and with very little charity, flashed her a look that produced instantaneous silence from her twin. Tyler wanted to laugh out loud, but didn't want to add to Amy's embarrassment. He loved the innocence in her eyes, and the knowledge that she'd spent as restless a night as he had gave him even more confidence that she was the woman to end his searching. Confident that God would show him in time, Tyler knew he could wait. After all, he'd waited this long.

"Ladies, if you'll take your seats, I'll start the service," he said with a tender glance at Amy.

Amy immediately relaxed. His look was almost apologetic. She couldn't figure out if the apology was for her sister's comments or for his actions the night before, but either way, he was kind to care. Amy had never known a man to be so considerate of her feelings.

The congregation fell silent when Tyler stepped forward. He'd refused to stand in the back of a wagon, as one person had suggested, for he knew he needed no extra height while he preached. Instead, he'd asked only for a small table upon which he could place his Bible.

Amy couldn't help but notice the way he cradled the beloved book. She could tell by the way he caressed the cover with his large calloused hands that this Bible meant the world to him. It was clearly his life's blood, and confirmation came in the powerful words which followed.

"People without God are nothing," he began. "They have no purpose, no destiny—no life. They are useless in matters of importance and worthless tasks are all they know." The words rang out loud and clear, and no one, not even the children, said a word.

"People without God doesn't know which way to walk, or where they're bound. They don't have even the slightest solid path to follow and they are lost from the one road that matters." Tyler's intense stare moved from person to person. As he made eye contact with the community people, he could see whose life was saved and whose wasn't, by the looks on their faces. Some met his stare with a confident nod; those were souls who'd clearly accepted the truth of the Word. Other's seemed to squirm uncomfortably at the contact he made; these knew the truth of the words but weren't following them. One or two stared in disinterest and seemed preoccupied with other things; these souls were not yet open to the urging of God's Spirit or they'd chosen to ignore Him altogether.

When Tyler's eyes fell upon Angie, she straightened up in her seat and gave him a sweet smile. And then his eyes moved on to Amy. She was fairly on the edge of her seat, so hungry to hear the Word preached that she was oblivious to the fact that this was the same man who'd held her so intimately the night before. When Tyler's gaze met her eyes, he saw the need there. A need for God's word—a need to hear the truth reconfirmed, over and over. A woman after the heart of God.

Tyler pulled his eyes from her face before continuing. "Jesus said, in John 14:6, 'I am the way, the truth, and the life. No man cometh unto the Father, but by me,'" Tyler paused to let the words sink in.

"Think about it folks. Jesus made it real plain to the people of His time. But not only that; He made it simple and clear for the people of our time and for those whose time has not yet come. He's the only way. He's the only truth. He's the only life!"

The richness of his booming voice seemed to penetrate Amy, and she began to tremble from the very power of the hand of God upon this man. Tyler Andrews was clearly God's chosen servant. Several people around Amy murmured an "Amen", or "Hallelujah", but Amy remained fixed and silent. At that moment, she longed only to be nourished upon the Word.

"You all have a purpose in life," Tyler was saying, "and if you aren't living that purpose, you're missing a very special pleasure that God has reserved just for you. Some of you know that purpose, others don't. Some of you share a common purpose, and others of you are fixed upon a solitary path. But that purpose, that way God has established for you, leads everyone in the same direction. It leads to His arms and to His very heart. It leads you home."

The silence that fell was nearly deafening. Amy felt a warmth spread through her body as she thought of walking home to God. Yes, that's exactly how it was to be a Christian. You had a definite direction and a path that was sure. Then at the end of your way, you got to go home to the Father—your very own Father.

"Do you know the way home?" Tyler asked the congregation. "Is your path clearly marked? It's a simple step to the right path and your Heavenly Father is waiting at the other end of the road. He's waiting for you to come home."

Tyler offered salvation through Jesus to the residents of Deer Ridge, and Amy was deeply moved by the sight of grown men weeping in their acceptance. Women who'd struggled under the heavy burden of the loneliness and tension of prairie life gave up their loads and placed them at the feet of God.

After Tyler closed, the congregation lingered to sing and praise God. People gave their testimonies, stories Amy had never heard, stories which blessed her heart and gave her hope and reason to also praise God. This was why the calling of the faithful was so important. This was the fellowship of God's people that she had so sorely missed. These were her brothers and sisters, and how dear they were to her, how rich the love she felt for each one.

The gathering turned into a celebration again. After the services, leftovers from the night before were joined with a few new foods, and lunch was served. While they ate, the residents of Deer Ridge urged Tyler to return to their community as soon as possible.

"We've missed having a man of God in our town," the town's schoolmaster, Marvin Williams, said, shaking Tyler's hand. "When you come back, we'll use the schoolhouse for the services." There was a hearty confirmation from the crowd that had gathered around Tyler.

Tyler took out a small black book and pencil. "I can be here in three weeks on a Saturday. That's when I'll be back in this part of the district again."

"Then it's settled," someone called out from the group. The murmured affirmation was enough to confirm the entire matter.

As families began to pick up their belongings and wagons were repacked, Amy couldn't help but feel a sadness to see them go. Sometimes the isolation of the prairie wore heavy on her soul.

Rebuking herself for her attitude, Amy realized that she'd have little time to feel sorry for herself with all the work left to do to get ready for winter. Mentally, she began a list.

November was always butchering month. The men would be getting together to butcher the hogs. This was planned for the first true cold spell, and Amy knew that wouldn't be far off. Then there was the matter of the apple preserves, jellies, and butters that she still needed to put up before the apples went bad. Then they'd can some of the meat, smoke the rest, and make soap with the fat.

Amy moved around, picking up messes whereever they caught her eye, and continued to think of the things she needed to take care of in the weeks to come. She was so lost in thought that she hadn't been aware of Tyler's watchful eye.

When she looked up, though, her eyes immediately met his. He stood casually against a cottonwood tree, arms folded across his chest, a gleam in his eye. Amy glanced around, wondering where Angie was and why she wasn't captivating Tyler's attention.

A smile spread across Tyler's face, as if he could read her thoughts. She blushed and quickly lowered her eyes to the work at hand. Tyler, however, wouldn't allow her to get away that easy.

"I'd like to have a minute or two alone with you," he

said, taking the dirty plates from her hand. He placed them back on the table and turned to her. "That is, if you don't object."

Amy felt her pulse quicken. "Of course I don't object," she answered. Her hands were trembling as she wiped them on her apron and allowed Tyler to direct her away from the crowded farmyard.

"I suppose you'll be leaving soon." She hated to say goodbye, but she knew it was inevitable.

"Yes," Tyler answered.

They walked past the new barn, and Amy realized that Tyler was leading her back to the orchard. As soon as they were well away from the noisy neighbors, he slipped his hand from Amy's arm and into her hand. They continued to walk in silence for several moments until they came to the spot where they'd kissed the night before.

"Amy." Tyler paused to look down into her face. "I have to say something to you before I go."

Amy felt her stomach tighten and her legs began to tremble. "All right."

He abruptly dropped his hand and turned away from her, as if he had something to say that was painful and distasteful. Amy twisted her hands together, burdened by the thought that perhaps he wanted to reprimand her for the night before. She waited, head bowed and hands clenched, while Tyler seemed to contemplate something of extreme importance. When he finally turned back to her, Amy couldn't bring herself to face him. She kept her head lowered.

He reached out and gently lifted her face. When he did, he saw her cheeks were damp with tears. "What's this all about?" he whispered softly.

Amy choked back a sob, certain that God was going to

tell her Tyler Andrews was not the man for her. "I, uh. . ., I'm sorry," was all she could manage to say.

"Sorry? For what?"

Amy began to wring her hands, but Tyler took one of her small hands in each of his larger ones. "Have I offended you?" he questioned gently.

"Never!" Amy dared to look up into his compassionate eyes. The worried expression she saw there touched her heart, and silently she wished there was an easy way to apologize.

"Then what's the trouble?" Tyler asked.

"I was just afraid that *I'd* offended *you*," Amy finally managed to say.

Tyler chuckled softly. "And how, my dear Amy, do you imagine you might have accomplished this offense?"

Amy swallowed hard, unable to concentrate on anything but the touch of his hands on hers. "I thought maybe you brought me out here to talk about last night."

"I did."

"Then I was right. I'm really sorry about acting so loose with you." Amy licked her lips nervously. "I'm really not generally so forward. In fact, mother worried that I'd never take an interest in anyone. Honestly, that was my first kiss." Amy's honesty was telling Tyler a great deal more than she'd expected.

She continued to try to make amends. "Just please forgive me. I know you're a minister and all, but I guess I was just, well. . ." her words drifted into silence. She really had no excuse for what she'd done.

"You think I brought you out here for a comeuppance? Is that it?" Tyler asked in a serious tone.

"Yes." Amy hung her head.

Tyler gently brushed his finger against her closed lips.

"I'm responsible for what happened last night," he whispered. "Yes, it was a bit forward and I, not you, am the one who should apologize." He broke into a broad smile. "But I am glad that I was the first one to kiss you and," he added with a certainty that caused Amy to tremble anew, "I intend to be the only one who has that privilege."

Amy stared open-mouthed for a moment, but then the real meaning of Tyler's words sank in. She smiled, realizing Tyler wasn't upset with her at all.

"You look so charming when you smile," he whispered, tracing the line of her jaw with his finger. "Then again, you look wonderful even when you aren't smiling."

Amy cocked her head slightly to one side and put her hands on her hips. "Just what are you up to, Tyler Andrews?"

"I just wanted a chance to tell you a proper goodbye." He grinned.

"Goodbye, then," Amy said with a hint of laughter in her voice. She started to walk away, but Tyler reached out and pulled her back. Amy couldn't suppress a giggle. Her heart was suddenly light; Tyler was obviously as interested in her as she was in him.

"Oh, no, you don't," he said. "You must be a more mischievous person than I thought. I thought Angie was the manipulative one, always teasing with people's feelings and such."

Amy stiffened and felt her muscles go rigid. Her smile was replaced with a look of serious intent. "I wasn't teasing with your feelings, Tyler."

"I know," he replied soberly and added, "and neither am I."

"Three weeks is a long time," Amy murmured.

Tyler took her face in his weathered hands and looked

deeply into her eyes for what seemed an eternity. "Three weeks is just a heartbeat, Amy. Just a heartbeat."

five

By the end of the first week, Amy had put up seven quarts of applesauce, fifteen quarts of apple preserves, and twenty-four pints of apple butter. She also helped her father and mother with the butchered hogs. She stuffed sausage casings until she thought she'd drop, and she helped her mother hang so much meat in the smokehouse that not a spot was left to put even one more ham. When all that was done, she and her mother canned enough meat and vegetables to bulge the pantry shelves.

The second week she missed Tyler more than she had the first, but Amy plunged into anything that kept her mind occupied and her hands busy. She ripped rags into strips and braided them into rugs, then worked in a fury through her mother's great pile of mending, much to the amazement of everyone. She counted the days down and then dissected the days into hours and counted those too.

Taking advantage of a clear but cold day, Amy was boiling a kettle of lye for soap, when Angie came sashaying through the yard.

"Ma wants me to see if you need any help." Angie pushed out her lips in a pout.

Amy knew better than to solicit Angie's help. Angie was hopelessly clumsy at most every household task. Ma had said on more than one occasion that they'd all be lucky if Angie did move back east to a big city with servants.

"No, Angie. I was about to add the grease and you know

49

how careful I have to be with the amount. I'd rather just work alone."

"Good," Angie said with a sudden smile. "Do you realize that Tyler will be returning in little more than a week? I've asked Ma to help me make a new skirt. I needed one anyway, but I think it will be glorious to wear it for Tyler the first time."

Amy bit back a angry retort and poured grease into the caldron. She couldn't stand the way her sister was acting these days. Most all their lives the twins had been comfortably close—not like people thought twins ought to be, but close enough. They really had very little in common, but still a bond had tied them together. Now, though, that bond seemed to be fraying.

"And Betsey said she heard him telling Randy that he was quite taken with me," Angie said, dancing around the caldron to keep warm.

Amy's head snapped up. "What did you say?"

"I said, Tyler told Randy that he was quite taken with me," Angie repeated.

"He said that?" Amy nearly forgot to stir the soap.

"Well, he didn't use my name, but Betsey said that Randy was certain he meant me." Angie ignored the look of displeasure on Amy's face.

Amy wiped the perspiration from her brow and continued to work over the fire. She was certain Tyler hadn't meant Angie. How could he after the things he'd said? She wished she could ask Angie for more details without arousing suspicion, but Angie would pick up her interest in a flash. Besides, Amy reminded herself, Tyler had voiced his own interests and they certainly did not include Angie.

Angie was growing bored with Amy's lack of attention.

"I'm going back into the house. Ma will be here to help shortly," she finally said and turned to walk away. Then she stopped abruptly and came back to where Amy was working with the wooden tubs for cutting the soap. "I almost forgot, Ma said that we'll need about ten dozen bars of hard soap. She wants to give some to the Riggs since Anna Beth is due to have her baby any day. All the women in town have agreed to take care of something and we get to provide soap."

Amy nodded and tried to mentally calculate how much rosin she'd need to add to make the soap set up and how much soft soap she'd have left over for their other house cleaning needs. "Tell Ma by my best calculation that'll leave us with five barrels of house soap."

Angie nodded and went on her way, while Amy still worried about Angie's attraction to Tyler. She'd never really cared before about her sister's flirtatious ways, but now with Tyler in the picture her sister grated on her nerves like fingernails on a slate. What if Angie ruined everything for her? What if Tyler ended up liking Angie's fun-loving nature more than Amy's quieter one? Maybe she should tell Angie that she cared for Tyler. Maybe then Angie would leave well enough alone.

Amy remembered then a verse from the Bible: "The Lord shall fight for you, and ye shall keep thy peace." The words of Exodus 14:14 seemed to haunt Amy throughout the day and by nightfall she was thoroughly convinced that she should hold her tongue and say nothing to her sister about her feelings for Tyler.

❧

When only two days remained until Tyler's return, Angie made an announcement that stunned Amy into an even deeper silence. "I've decided that I'm going to marry Tyler."

Amy slapped the bread dough she'd been about to place into pans onto the floury board and began to knead it some more. She thrust her fingers deep into the soft mass again and again; Angie had stirred an anger inside her that Amy didn't want to acknowledge.

"I see," she managed to say at last.

Angie pulled up a chair, certain her sister would want to hear all the details. "His parents still live in Kansas City and that's perfect for me. I could go and live with them and maybe I could even convince Tyler to get a big church in the city and quit the circuit. I just know I'd love Kansas City."

"What about Tyler?" Amy found herself asking against her better judgement.

Angie laughed. For her, the situation was as fun as a good game of croquet. "Why, I'd love Tyler too. What did you think, silly goose, that I'd marry a man I didn't love? I think Tyler is one of the greatest men I've ever known and I just know we'd be right for each other."

Just then Dora Carmichael entered the kitchen to find Amy nearly destroying the bread dough. "Amy, what in the world are you doing?"

Amy looked down at the sorry mess. "Sorry, Ma, I was a bit preoccupied."

Angie flashed Amy a look that demanded silence regarding their discussion, and Amy said nothing more.

"Mercy," Dora said as she pulled out a chair and sat down. "I'm feeling a bit peaked."

Amy placed a hand on her mother's forehead. "Ma, you've got a fever. You go on up to bed and I'll bring you some sassafras tea." Amy pulled her mother to her feet.

"I hate to leave all this work to you girls." Dora knew full well the load would fall to Amy.

"Nonsense, Ma. You're sick and you have to get to bed before the shakes set in. Do you think it's the ague?" Amy remembered her mother's bouts with the sickness.

"Can't rightly say that it feels that way, but time will tell. Better get the quinine anyway." Dora headed toward the stairs. "Angie, you make yourself helpful," she called over her shoulder.

Angie grimaced. "Ma must think I don't do a thing around here," she pouted, but Amy had no time to care. She had to tend to her mother, for she knew that prevention was crucial here on the frontier. If they were to have any chance at all of heading off a bad bout of ague or a serious fever of some other nature, Amy knew they'd need to work fast.

৯

When Saturday morning arrived, Dora was still sick. She'd suffered with the shakes and fever for over two days, but Amy felt certain her mother was getting better now. The only problem, however, was that this was the day Tyler would preach in Deer Ridge, and Amy could not leave her mother alone.

When Charles came in to check on his wife, Amy assured her father that she'd see to everything. "Just go on to the services, Pa, and tell everyone hello for me." Amy tried not to sound too disappointed.

Angie had already put a deep dent in Amy's sense of well-being by prancing through the house wearing her new blue plaid wool skirt. Every other word was Tyler this, and Tyler that, and Amy thought she'd scream before the buckboard finally pulled down the drive for town, with Angie securely blanketed at their father's side.

When her mother was dozing comfortably, Amy went to stoke the fire in the stove. She couldn't stop the tears that flowed down her cheeks when she thought of missing Tyler's service. How cruel life was and how unfair.

She tried to pray, but her heart wasn't in it. Instead, she found herself whispering over and over, "Help me, Father, to understand. Help me to understand."

By mid-day, Dora was feeling well enough to sit in a chair for a while and take some beef broth. Amy knew this was a good sign and tried to feel more cheerful. She tried to chat light-heartedly with her mother, but Dora could sense that something was amiss. Amy assured her mother that nothing was wrong.

When the hall clock chimed four, she helped Dora back to bed and went downstairs to tend to the other household needs. Soon, she heard first the wagon, then Angie's animated laughter. Amy was anxious to ask her father what Tyler had preached on and hurried out to the barn, meeting Angie half way.

"How's Mama doing?" Angie's voice was filled with real concern. No one could accuse Angie of not loving her family, despite her absorption with her own self.

"Much better," Amy answered. "She's napping now, but she was up earlier and even ate a little."

Relief passed across Angie's face. "I think I'll peek in on her and then I'm going to bake some muffins," she said and walked past her sister toward the house.

"Why in the world would you want to bake muffins, Angie? You know you hate to cook."

Angie whirled on her heel and put her finger to her lips, indicating that Amy should be quiet. Amy cocked her head slightly and then realized that her father was talking to someone in the barn. Angie hurried into the house, while Amy made her way to the barn in time to find her father and Tyler sharing a hearty laugh.

Amy's mouth dropped open. She had no idea he would accompany her father back to the farm and she looked down at her dress, realizing that it was stained and smudged from the ashes in the fireplace. She knew she must look a fright, but Tyler smiled warmly at her as though he'd genuinely missed her.

"How's your Ma doing?" Charles asked Amy when he'd finished hanging up the tack.

"Much better, Pa. She's resting, but wanted to see you when you got home." Amy tried to keep her voice even. In truth, her nerves were rattled, all because of the smiling giant who stood behind her father.

"You've done a good job by your Ma, Amy. I'm deeply grateful for your love of her," Charles said, reaching out to give his daughter a warm embrace. "I'm going to go see your Ma now. Tyler, if you need anything, I'm sure this little lady will be happy to accommodate you."

Amy blushed a deep scarlet, and when her father was out of earshot, Tyler let out a hearty laugh. "Well now," he said with a teasing tone, "how about accommodating me with the same kind of greeting your Pa got?"

He crossed the distance between them and lifted Amy into the air to whirl her in a circle. "My, but I've missed you. How in the world can you stand there so calm and quiet? I wanted to give out a yell when I saw you there."

Amy had to laugh. "Put me down, Tyler." She said his name with pleasure. How she loved this man! Now that she saw him again, she admitted the fact to herself. She chided herself that she might be feeling a mere childish crush, but her heart told her otherwise.

Tyler allowed her feet to touch the ground, and his hands left her waist. How he'd missed her! But had she missed him too? Tyler couldn't help but wonder. She seemed interested enough; she always responded positively to his touch, and she was honest to a fault. He knew he'd have only to ask her how she felt, and she'd no doubt spill her feelings. But could she love me, could she really love me, Tyler wondered to himself, the way I love her?

"So." Amy pulled away from Tyler's hold. Somehow she felt safer with some distance between them. "Why did you come to the farm today? I suppose Angie wouldn't have it any other way."

"Your sister does make it hard to say no," Tyler laughed.

Amy frowned, and Tyler couldn't help but notice the furrows that suddenly lined her forehead. She had been all laughing and smiles one minute and now she looked sad, almost miserable. Tyler had no way of knowing that Amy was contemplating Angie's plans to marry him.

A scream came suddenly from the house. Tyler and Amy whirled and ran across the yard. Smoke was pouring out of the kitchen door, and Angie stood screaming for help.

"Something's burning!" she exclaimed, nearly hysterical. "Oh, Amy, do something!"

Tyler and Amy shared a brief look, and then Amy moved past her sister into the smoke-filled kitchen. "Didn't you think to check the oven before you fired up the stove? I had your supper warming there and now it's burned." Amy threw a look back at Angie. "Don't just stand there crying, Angie, open the windows." She looked past her sister to the towering man who stood behind her and added, "Tyler, would you go upstairs and tell Pa what happened? I'll take care of this." She took a potholder in one hand and covered her mouth with the other in order to ward off the smoke.

In a few minutes, Amy returned outside to deposit the hopelessly burned food. Angie soon joined her after opening the windows to let out the smoke. After the smoke had cleared, Amy went to work fixing them something else to eat, while Angie took the opportunity to court Tyler.

Amy tried not to feel angry about things, but it was difficult. She kept worrying that Angie was using Tyler and that somehow he would come to care more about her twin than about Amy. She attacked a ham, slicing off thick pieces to fry on the stove, all the while considering how frustrated she felt playing second fiddle to her more rambunctious sister.

When she had mixed up a batch of muffins, she started to relax a bit. If God wants you to have Tyler for a mate, she reminded herself, no amount of interference from Angie will matter.

Outside, Amy could hear the wind pick up and felt a chilly blast, cold enough to merit closing the windows. Placing the muffins securely into the oven and checking to make certain the temperature wasn't too hot, Amy went around the house closing the windows.

She had just walked into the front parlor when she heard Angie's voice. Apparently she had taken Tyler to the front porch swing in order to share her heart with him. "It must be wonderful to see so many different places, but don't you ever get lonely, Tyler?" Before Tyler could answer, Angie asked him a second question. "I mean, don't you ever think of getting married again?"

Amy felt her ire rising at her sister's brazen behavior. Angie was being totally improper, even if Amy *had* wondered the same things.

Tyler's laughter caught Amy's attention, however, and she found herself eavesdropping to hear the answer to Angie's questions. Did Tyler get lonely? Did he want another wife? Angie wasn't as patient as Amy, and she prodded Tyler to speak. "Well?"

"I do get lonely, Angie. These open prairie plains are enough to do that to any man. And, yes, I do plan to marry again."

"I see." Angie thought a moment and then said, "Why don't we go into the parlor, Tyler? I'm getting a chill out here, what with the sun going down."

Amy heard the creak of the porch swing as it's occupants got up. She had no recourse but to leave the parlor windows open and go out the back way. She wasn't about to have Tyler or Angie catch her listening to their conversation.

She hurried to the kitchen and pulled the golden brown muffins from the oven. They were plump, just barely crisp on the tops, and Amy knew they were some of the finest she'd ever made. She hurriedly placed them on the table and added bowls of plum jelly and freshly churned butter. Then she turned her attention to the ham steaks and put some potatoes on to boil.

Soon the table began to take on the look of a proper supper, and Amy felt satisfied that she'd worked through her anger. She loved her sister and hated to think anything could come between them.

Amy was just about to call her family to supper when her father appeared in the kitchen doorway. Behind him were Tyler and Angie.

"It's getting mighty late, Tyler. Why don't you plan on staying the night with us?" Charles Carmichael invited.

"Oh, do say yes, Tyler," Angie gushed. "I do so want to hear more about Kansas City."

Amy glanced up, her soft brown eyes betraying her own desire for Tyler to stay. With a chuckle, Tyler sniffed the air. "How can I pass up the opportunity for such great cooking and company? My schedule's pretty tight, but I'd be happy to stay. Thank you."

"Well, it's settled then." Charles smiled. "I'll ready a room for you."

six

Amy had more than her fill of Angie's fussing over Tyler. Angie hadn't really done anything improper, but Amy felt jealous of the control and confidence her twin boasted.

After clearing the supper dishes and putting the kitchen in order, Amy decided to retire to her room and leave Tyler to Angie's wiles. Going quietly to check on her mother first, Amy found that Dora was feeling much better. She gave her mother a dose of quinine and a drink of cold water and then sought out the sanctuary of her room. She was contemplating her feelings for Tyler and the promise she felt God had given her about waiting, when a knock sounded at her door.

"Yes?" Amy called.

"Amy, Carl Riggs is downstairs," said her father's voice from the other side of the door. Amy opened the door to reveal his worried face. "It's the baby, Amy. Carl thinks that Anna Beth is dying in childbirth. He needs you to come midwife 'cause Doc is out of town."

Amy smiled, trying to ease her father's worry. "Of course I'll go, Pa. But every man I've ever known thought his wife was dying in childbirth. It's probably nothing at all."

Charles placed his hand on his daughter's arm. "Carl says there's a great deal of blood, Amy."

Amy's expression changed immediately. "I'll get the birthing bag. Will you saddle the horse for me?"

"I can take you in the wagon if you like."

"No, there won't be time. I'll have to ride like all get

60

out as it is." Amy pulled on a heavy coat she used for outdoor chores. "I'll be downstairs in just a minute."

Charles nodded and hurried to saddle the horse for his daughter.

Amy grabbed what her mother had dubbed, "the birthing bag." It held the supplies the Carmichael women had found useful over the years during childbirth chores. Amy knew it had a collection of herbs for easing pain and bleeding, as well as the routine tools necessary for bringing new life into the world.

She fairly flew down the stairs and ran headlong into Tyler. She was startled to find his hands reaching out to steady her.

"I think I'd better come too," he said solemnly. "If the woman is truly dying, she may need me too."

Amy nodded, her eyes worried. "It doesn't sound good any time there's a lot of bleeding." She glanced around the hallway for Mr. Riggs. "Where's Carl?"

"He went with your father to the barn. Come on and I'll carry this for you." Tyler took the birthing bag.

Angie stood by the door, looking helpless and without purpose. Amy turned to her, realizing her discomfort. "Angie, you'll need to care for Ma. I gave her the quinine just a few minutes ago, but you might want to look in on her shortly." With those few words, Amy redeemed her sister's obvious lack of nursing skill. With that behind her, Amy lifted her skirts and ran for the barn.

❧

The Riggs lived in a two room soddy about two miles from the Carmichael farm. Amy was off her horse and flying through the soddy door before the men had even managed to dismount. "Anna Beth," she called as she entered the bedroom.

Amy was shocked by the blood-drenched sheets and bedding. Anna Beth had to be bleeding a great deal to have soaked through the quilted blankets that had been placed on top of her.

"Amy Carmichael," a weak voice called out, "is that you?"

"It is, Anna Beth. Ma's sick in bed, so I'm here to help you with the birthing. We need to get these wet things off you." Amy started removing the quilts as Tyler and Carl entered the room.

"Dear God," Carl moaned at the sight of the blood.

"Carl, I need you to get water boiling on the stove. Then I want you to cut me some strips from any extra sheets you have. It's really important. I know you'd rather be here with Anna Beth, but I need you out there." Amy motioned toward the kitchen. "Can you do it?"

Carl nodded, almost relieved to leave the sight of his dying wife. Tyler stood fast in the doorway. "What can I do to help?"

"Oh, Tyler, we need to get her out of all this blood. Can you lift her while I cut the nightgown away?" Amy pulled the last of the bloody quilts away.

"Just show me what to do."

Anna Beth's weak voice barely whimpered a protest, as the contractions ripped through her abdomen. Amy could tell by the flow of blood that the birth of Anna Beth's child would also be the death of her.

"Anna Beth," Amy called to the barely conscious woman. Amy shook her head, for in truth Anna Beth was barely a woman. Anna Beth Riggs was only sixteen, but on the frontier, adulthood came early and birthing was the ultimate arrival of womanhood.

Amy wiped the woman's head with a cool cloth. She

knew she could do very little for her. Amy's only real hope was to save the baby and pray that God would help the mother. But in order to accomplish even the delivery, Amy was going to have to pull the child from the birthing canal.

"Anna Beth, your baby is having a hard time being born. I need to help him," Amy said softly. She glanced up to meet Tyler's intense stare. He seemed concerned for Amy's well-being, as well as for the dying woman. Amy shook her head at him, for her own feelings could not possibly matter at a time like this.

"Amy, save my baby, please! Do whatever you must," Anna Beth whispered and then turned to Tyler. "Pastor, will you pray for us?"

"Of course, Anna Beth." Tyler took hold of the woman's hand. "Father, we lift up your daughter, Anna Beth. She's fought a hard fight, Lord, and we ask that you ease her burden and give her rest. We ask for the safe delivery of her child and your healing touch upon both. Steady Amy's hands to do what she must, that we might all bring you glory. In Jesus's name, amen."

Amy felt warmed by the prayer. She placed a hand on the struggling woman and patted her reassuringly. "Anna Beth, you just rest a minute. I need to talk to Tyler and tell him what I need him to do. I'll just be right at the end of the bed, so you won't be alone." The woman nodded, and Amy motioned Tyler to the foot of the bed.

"This won't be easy, Tyler. I'll need you to hold her down and still. I'll have to reach up inside and pull the baby down. It's not a pretty sight and it won't be pleasant work. Can you help me? I know Carl won't be able to stand it."

Tyler took hold of Amy's upper arms and held her firmly

for a moment. "I'll stay by your side no matter the cost. You can count on me to be there for you." Tyler's words somehow seemed a promise of something more.

Amy nodded. "We must work fast or we'll lose the baby too. It may already be too late."

Tyler and Amy took their places at the bedside, and Amy explained to Anna Beth that she had to hold as still as possible. "Tyler is going to help you, Anna Beth. It won't be very easy for you and it's going to hurt." Anna Beth nodded and accepted Tyler's hands upon her shoulders.

Amy rolled up a washing cloth and gave it to Anna Beth. "Bite down on this." Obediently, the woman heeded her instructions.

At Tyler's nod, Amy went to work. For the first time since their arrival, Anna Beth screamed, and then she lost consciousness. Amy worked unsuccessfully to rotate the breech positioned baby and finally managed to pull the child out, bottom first.

The baby boy was stillborn.

Amy glanced down at Anna Beth, who was just starting to stir. The blood was flowing even harder now, and Amy knew no amount of packing would ever keep Anna Beth alive.

Anna Beth's eyes fluttered open. She looked first to Tyler, then at Amy. Amy pulled out a soft flannel blanket that Anna Beth had made for her baby and wrapped the child lovingly in it's folds. She talked gently to the baby, as if it were alive.

Tyler stood by in utter amazement, not certain what Amy was doing. He watched in silence as Amy washed the tiny, red face of the infant and smoothed back the downy black hair on his head.

"Anna Beth," Amy said as she brought the infant to his mother. "Your son is a might worried."

Anna Beth perked up at the words that she had a son. "What is it, Amy? Can I hold him?"

"Of course you can." Amy placed the small bundle in Anna Beth's arms. "Does he have a name?"

"Carl Jr.," Anna Beth whispered, trying feebly to stroke the baby softness of her son's cheek.

"Anna Beth," Amy whispered as she stroked the woman's hair, "Carl Jr. is afraid to be without you. He wants to know if it would be all right to go on to Heaven and wait for you there."

Tears fell down Anna Beth's cheeks, but Amy's remained dry. Her eyes revealed her pain, however, and Tyler longed to take her away from the death scene in the Riggs' bedroom.

"That would be fine, little boy," Anna Beth murmured to the baby. She cupped his cheek with her hand. "Mama will be right there. You go on ahead. Mama's coming soon." She glanced up and smiled at Amy. Her eyes were filled with a sad knowledge, but also with peace. "Thank you, Amy." She pulled her son close and closed her eyes. She sighed, glad that the pain was over. And then Anna Beth joined her son in Heaven.

❧

For several moments, no one said a word. Amy continued to smooth Anna Beth's hair, unmindful of her action. Tyler reached out and took Amy's hand from across the bed.

"Yea, though I walk through the valley of the shadow of death, I will fear no evil: for thou art with me," he recited.

Amy looked up into Tyler's eyes, grateful for his comforting presence. This was only her second time to deal with death in childbirth, and it wasn't any easier than the last time.

"Thank you, Tyler," she said. Letting go of his hand, she squared her shoulders. "I'll get the bodies ready for burial. Will you tell Carl?"

"Of course."

৯৯

Nearly two hours later, Amy and Tyler left the stunned Carl and rode back to the Carmichael farm. They'd both tried to convince Carl to come back with them, but he wanted to be near his family. He'd requested that Tyler perform the funeral the next day and Tyler readily agreed.

At nearly two o'clock in the morning, they made their way across the open prairie. Amy was quieter than ever, and Tyler knew her mind was on Anna Beth and the baby.

"Child birth is a risky thing," he said. "I sometimes wonder how a woman can bear a normal delivery, much less as much pain as that woman had to endure tonight."

"It's the joy of the child to come," Amy said absently. She smiled sadly. "I know I'm not a mother, but I've heard enough to tell their story. I think maybe it's the things that cost the most pain that are the things most worth having, the things that bring us the most joy."

"You believe that to be true about children?" Tyler's question seemed louder than he'd intended, somehow amplified by the vast expanse of the open plains.

"I suppose I do," Amy murmured.

"You only suppose? Don't you plan to have children, Amy?" After what they had witnessed tonight, he wouldn't blame her if she said no.

"Beyond today," Amy said, "I don't have any plans." She tried to laugh, making light of her life long doctrine.

"Maybe that's because you've never had the right

person to plan with."

"Maybe," Amy admitted. "But I feel God wants me to just take a day at a time. I think it keeps me better focused than looking at the big picture."

"What do you mean?"

Amy pulled her coat collar around her throat. The night had turned cold and a shadowy ring had formed around the moon. The air tasted like snow.

She could tell that Tyler's eyes were still on her. He was waiting for an answer to his question, and throwing caution to the wind, Amy decided to be honest with him. "Angie always has plans a plenty. She revels in them like some people glory in a large account of money. Angie knows what she wants in life, or at least she thinks she does. She wants to live in the city and have the world eat out of her hand. And believe me, Tyler," Amy paused to look at Tyler's silhouetted profile, "she's used to getting what she wants."

"But what about you?" Tyler asked, frustrated by this talk of Angie when Amy's feelings were what concerned him. "What do you want?"

Amy smiled. "I want whatever God wants for me. I'm not always very patient, but I know His promises are rich. I don't want to miss out on a single one of His gifts."

Tyler's mouth curved. "That's a bit evasive, don't you think?"

"Perhaps."

The lights from the front room of the Carmichael farm were now in view. Just a few more minutes and they would be home. Amy felt the weariness deep in her bones. She felt as if she could sleep forever.

Silently, she braved a glance at the man who rode by her side. She was surprised to find him watching her with an unreadable expression on his face. Amy offered a weak smile.

"I'm glad you were with me tonight," she whispered and turned toward the barn.

Tyler sat back thoughtfully in the saddle. She was quite a woman, this Amy Carmichael, he thought to himself. In his heart, he knew she was much more to him than just another member of his flock.

seven

Charles Carmichael took one look at their faces and then shook his head sadly. He took his daughter's hand in his. "You gave it your best and God was with you, child. You mustn't blame yourself."

Amy leaned against her father and sighed. "I know, Pa. We tried to talk Carl into coming home with us, but he didn't want to leave them."

Charles nodded. "I don't think I would've left your Ma either. He'll have to work through this in his own way. No one can grieve for you, Amy. No matter how many others shed their tears, the pain is still your own. We'll keep him in our prayers, and I'll ride over tomorrow and see how I can help."

"Thanks, Pa." Amy was too close to tears to say anything more.

With the horses cared for, Charles led them back to the house. "I'll show you where we put your things, Tyler." Tyler nodded and gave Amy a quick glance before following her father up the stairs.

"Don't forget to turn down the lamp, Amy," Charles called over his shoulder.

"I won't. Good night, Pa." Almost as an afterthought, she added, "Good night, Tyler."

ada

In the empty downstairs, the silence fell around her like a cloak. Amy felt drained and cold in the aftermath of what had taken place. She went to the front room and stoked

69

up the fire before easing her weight onto the sofa. Staring into the flames, she felt her composure crumble.

Tears fell down her cheeks, until she was sobbing quietly into her hands. Why did bad things happen to people who loved God? It seemed so harsh. So unfair. Why, if a person put their trust in the Lord, didn't He relieve their suffering and keep them from the horrors of the world?

Without warning, Amy felt herself being swept to her feet. Tyler's warm fingers took her hands from her face. Staring up at him with red eyes, Amy's tears began anew.

"Hush, it will be all right." He pulled her into his arms. Amy laid her face against his broad chest and sobbed.

Her tears raged for several minutes, while Tyler waited patiently for her to regain control. He stroked her hair and whispered over and over in her ear that it would be all right. The words, though plain and simple, were a comfort, not only for what they said, but because of who said them.

"I'm sorry," Amy murmured, finally feeling able to speak. Tyler's arms were still around her, and she wasn't ready yet to pull away from the safety she felt there.

"Don't be." Tyler pulled her with him to sit on the sofa. "You can't bear the pain for all the world."

"I try so hard to be strong. I want so much to be of some use to God," Amy whispered. "I guess sometimes I'm just not cut out for His work."

"Nonsense." Tyler's firmness surprised Amy. "God knows what each man and woman can bear. He knows how your heart breaks for those who suffer—but He knows too how He can use that pain in you to do the work of His kingdom. If your heart wasn't so tender, the Lord wouldn't be able to use you so much."

"It just seems so unfair." Amy allowed Tyler to pull her

head against his shoulder. "There's a part of me that wants to cry out and ask why this thing has happened. There's even a part of me, I'm ashamed to say, that questions how God can allow folks to suffer so."

Tyler smiled, though Amy never saw it. Hadn't he himself had those questions, those doubts? "That's pretty normal, Amy. Everybody wonders at something, sometime."

"I don't know, Tyler." Amy pushed away to look him in the eye. "I feel so helpless. Life out here is so hard. Sometimes I wonder if Angie doesn't have the better idea—escape to the city and live a more protected life." Before Tyler could say a word, she continued, "But then, I see a sunrise across the open prairie or hear the coyotes when the moon is high, and I know I could never leave it. For all its unmerciful hardships, I'm at home here and here I'll stay."

The words brought a flood of emotion to Tyler's heart. For a moment he'd feared she'd tell him she planned to move away with the first man who offered her an easier life in the big city. Hadn't he just listened to that very plan from her sister's lips earlier in the day? Now, he felt relieved by Amy's declaration. He was more certain than ever that Amy Carmichael was the woman God intended him to marry.

Amy started to wipe her face on her apron but then noticed the blood stains. "Christ spilled his blood for us," she whispered. "Although He was a man, I think He must have understood the pain a woman feels in childbirth. He knew what it was like to bleed, to feel pain, to die while giving life to another. So why do I feel so discouraged and sad? That should be enough."

"It is enough," Tyler agreed. "Enough for our salvation

and reconciliation with God. But although our eternal life is safe and assured, that's no guarantee we won't run into pain and hardship in our everyday, physical life. Like everyone, we must endure hardships and trials, just as Jesus said we would. Remember?"

Amy frowned for a moment, trying to remember what scripture Tyler might be quoting. She shook her head when nothing came to mind and waited for Tyler to enlighten her.

"Jesus was preparing for His death when He told His disciples in John 16:33, 'In the world ye shall have tribulation; but be of good cheer; I have overcome the world.' He made it real clear that we will have trouble in this life of ours. But the good news is that He's already overcome anything the world can throw at us."

"That's all fine and well." Amy's lips pressed tight together. She sighed and then burst out, "Of course He overcame the world. He was God. He had the power and the ability to overcome anything He chose. I know it sounds selfish, but how does that help me? I still have to go through the trials and heartaches. How do I comfort myself or find ease from the pain when its Jesus that has overcome, not me?"

Tyler read the agony in her eyes. He touched her face gently. "Because He overcame, we have the power to do the same. When we accepted Him as Savior, He came into our hearts. He became one with us, and now we share in His life. We share His suffering—but we also share His triumph. That's why He told us to be of good cheer. We're a part of Him now, and that means we've already overcome. We just don't realize it sometimes."

Amy stared thoughtfully into the fire for a moment before nodding her head. "Of course," she whispered.

"That makes so much sense. How could I have thought He was being a braggart, when He was simply trying to bolster the disciples' courage?"

Tyler nodded. "That's right, Amy. He knew we wouldn't be able to bear the load alone. When He died on the cross, He bore the pain of the entire world. He knew all about Anna Beth and her little boy. And He knew how you would hurt tonight. He's already taken that load onto Himself. All you have to do now is let Him have it. You have to let go of the pain you're feeling." Tyler smiled. "It's a funny thing, but sometimes it's almost harder to trust God with the hard things in our life than it is to trust Him with the happier things. Believe me, I know."

Amy smiled and sat back against the sofa. "You make it so easy to understand. I think that's why I've missed having church and a regular minister so much. I read the Word every day, but so often its meaning eludes me. Thank you for being patient with me, Tyler."

"I think, Amy, that when it comes to you," Tyler reached for her hand, "that I have an infinite amount of patience." He looked into her face. "Maybe we could pray about this together."

"Yes, please." Sudden joy leapt up from the depths of Amy's pain. How often she had dreamed of a man with whom she could pray about the sorrows and troubles of the day. A man who truly sought God's heart for the hidden answers and meanings to life's questions.

They prayed together silently, and then each shared their petitions aloud. Amy felt as though a revival of sorts was taking place just for them. For hours, in spite of the fact that dawn was fast approaching, they sat and prayed, talking about the mercies of God and their hope for the future.

Finally, Amy couldn't stifle a yawn, and Tyler pulled her to her feet. "Come on, sleepy head. You've had a busy night and you'd best get some sleep. From the sounds of the wind outside, I wouldn't be surprised to find a foot of snow on the ground by morning."

Amy had to laugh as she cast a suspicious glance at the mantel clock. "It's going to have to snow mighty hard and fast in order to meet that demand. After all, it's nearly morning now."

Tyler chuckled and pulled her along with him toward the stairs. "It could snow three feet by daylight, I wouldn't care one bit. I think I might rather enjoy being snowed in with you, Amy Carmichael."

❧

Tyler's words very nearly came true. First light greeted the Carmichael farm with a raging blizzard that dumped snow on top of snow, burying everything in a blanket of white.

Dora was up and feeling better when Charles returned from the barn and morning chores. "My," she exclaimed, brushing snow off his shoulders, "but you look frozen clear through!"

"It's a bad one out there." Charles shook the worst of the snow from his coat before hanging it up on the peg by the back door.

Angie burst into the kitchen all smiles and sunshine. "Good morning." She nearly sang the words. Glancing around for Tyler and Amy, she suddenly frowned. "Where is everybody?"

"Well, part of us are right here," Dora chided her daughter. "As for your sister and the pastor, I don't know."

"Well, I do." Charles stepped out of his wet boots. "They didn't get back until late last night. Anna Beth and the baby died."

"Oh no, Charles." Dora's stricken expression matched her husband's heavy heart. "Poor Carl. And poor Amy, having to deal with that alone. I should have been with her."

"She was pretty upset," Charles agreed, "but you know Amy. She held her ground. I wouldn't bother to wake up either one of them." He turned his eyes meaningfully toward Angie. "They need their rest."

Angie's lower lip threatened to quiver into a pout, but noting her father's stern expression, she managed to shrug her shoulders and leave well enough alone. Dora quickly put her daughter to work making bread, lest Angie change her mind and go about some type of noisy task. Angie was unhappy about the arrangement, but in light of her father's presence, she did as she was told.

Much to her surprise and pleasure, Angie found her patience rewarded when Tyler popped his head into the kitchen doorway nearly an hour later.

"Smells mighty good in here," he said with a grin toward Dora.

Dora was pushing bacon around the frying pan and looked up with a smile. "I thought you might be hungry. We've already eaten so you just make yourself comfortable at the table and tell me what you'd like to eat."

Tyler did as he was told and soon found Angie at his side. "Would you like some coffee?" she asked sweetly, eager to please.

"Sure would," he replied.

Dora barely managed to find out what Tyler wanted to eat, because Angie immediately monopolized him. Dora thought privately that their conversation seemed more like an interrogation than a conversation, with Angie in the role of interrogator.

At last Angie fell silent and sat looking dreamily at the man while he shoveled in forkfuls of Dora's scrambled eggs and potatoes. He squirmed a little under her steady stare, wishing she would turn her eyes somewhere else, but he didn't want to hurt her feelings. When she began her interrogation again, he tried to answer her questions when he could; if he didn't know the answer, she seemed just as content to move on to yet another subject.

At last, with hearty praise for Dora's fine cooking, Tyler moved from the kitchen. He allowed Angie to lead him to the front room where he'd spent most of the night talking to Amy. He couldn't help but think of her when Angie spread out her red calico skirt on the sofa and beckoned Tyler to join her there.

Leaning against the mantel, Tyler laughed. "I swear, Miss Angie, you have more energy than a woman ought to have."

Angie giggled and took his words as a compliment. "I do believe," she said, "that it's the company of one particular circuit rider that brings out the best in me."

This was the comment that a bleary-eyed Amy overheard from the doorway. She had thought to greet them both, but instead she backed away. Going to the kitchen, Amy found her mother taking fresh baked loaves of golden bread from their tins.

"Morning, Ma."

"Amy!" Dora set the pans aside. She hurried to her daughter's side and embraced her. "I'm so sorry about Anna Beth. I wish I could've been there to keep you from bearing that alone."

"I wasn't alone," Amy replied softly. "But I wish you'd been there too. I keep thinking that maybe it was my lack of experience that kept me from saving them."

Dora pulled back with a shake of her head. "No. You have no power over life and death, daughter. Only God has that. Besides, you've helped in more births than I can even name. Sometimes, no matter how skilled we might be, there's just nothing we can do. Anna Beth was a mere girl. Obviously the whole thing was too much for her. We have to trust she and her baby are both in God's hands."

Amy nodded. "Tyler stayed with me and helped. I was sure glad he was there. He helped me afterwards, too."

"Oh?" Dora felt hope flicker once again. She noticed the underlying softness to Amy's voice.

Amy nodded. "We stayed up and talked quite a while last night. Pa had shown Tyler to his room, while I decided to sit a spell and think on things. Pretty soon, though, I was blubbering like a baby—and Tyler was there to comfort me."

Dora hid her smile. "I see."

"Oh, Ma." Amy had a look in her eyes that left her mother no doubt as to her daughter's heart. "The best part was that he knew just what to say and then he prayed with me. Not just a short little prayer, but he really prayed. We must of talked to God for over an hour before we got it all said."

Dora squeezed Amy's shoulder and offered her a chair. Saying nothing, the two women sat down to the table, and Dora reached out her hand to take Amy's. Through the hallway drifted Angie's laughter, causing a frown to form on Amy's lips. Glancing up at her mother, Amy suddenly felt a kindred spirit with the woman who'd given her life. Dora smiled sympathetically, yet it was something more than just that.

"You know, don't you?" Amy questioned. "You know

what I'm feeling inside."

Dora nodded. "I've waited long enough to see you feel it. I knew when love came to you it would come like a rushing wind that knocked you off your feet and took away your breath."

"That's just how it is, too," Amy agreed. She found comfort in the fact that her mother knew her so well. Angie's boisterous laugh sounded again and Dora patted Amy's hand.

"Don't give it a second thought," she reassured. "If God is for you, who can be against you?"

Amy nodded, finding comfort in her mother's words.

❧

Hours later, the storm still showed no signs of abating. Tyler donned heavy boots and clothes to help Charles with the chores that wouldn't keep, while the womenfolk worked to keep the house warm and made sure that hot food and coffee were waiting.

Amy tried not to feel angry when Angie managed to control Tyler's time. She even bit back an angry remark when Angie set the table for dinner and placed Tyler between herself and Charles.

But by the time dinner was over, Amy had more than enough of Angie's brazen behavior and blatant designs. After washing the dishes, Amy managed to slip unnoticed to the back parlor. She sat down and considered her feelings in silence.

"I don't mean to be jealous, Lord. It's just that I can't hold a candle to my sister. I wish I could have more confidence like Angie, but it's just not me," she whispered aloud.

No, it isn't you, a voice seemed to whisper to her heart. Amy sat back and closed her eyes. Was God trying to speak to her? She relaxed for a moment, listening to the gentle silence, before feeling the need to say more. "Forgive me, Father. I'm sorry for being so mean-tempered. Forgive me." She felt a peace spread throughout her body. She wasn't Angie and she'd never be as lively and vivacious as her sister, but that didn't mean God hadn't given her qualities of merit that were all her own. Qualities that she already knew attracted Tyler.

"All right, Father." She folded her hands in her lap. "What do I do now?"

eight

"Are you avoiding me?"

Amy's head snapped up, surprised that Tyler had managed to get away from Angie long enough to seek her out. She tried to choose her words carefully before replying.

"No," she answered finally. "I just figured your attention was pretty well taken." She bit her lip, immediately wishing that she'd said something else.

"Your sister does have a way about her, doesn't she?" He laughed and came closer to where Amy sat.

"She always has," Amy replied rather flippantly. The anger was starting to surface again, making her feel she was a miserable failure after all her efforts to put her bad feelings aside.

Tyler suddenly became aware of Amy's feelings. She was obviously put out with the way Angie had monopolized his time. Why hadn't he seen it before? Reaching out, he pulled Amy to her feet and encircled her in his arms.

"Don't you know yet?" he whispered.

"Know what?" Amy's voice was a bit breathless. His actions had taken her by surprise.

"It's you I care about, not Angie. It's you who's captured my heart." Tyler's eyes pierced Amy's facade of strength. Her mouth formed an "O", but no sound escaped her lips. The sheepish curl of Tyler's lips widened into a full-fledged grin. "That's what I like best about you, Amy.

You're unassuming and so innocent. You have no idea what you do to me. Why, just one look at those big brown eyes and my heart does flip-flops inside. I love you, Amy."

Amy was grateful for the arms that held her. Her knees felt like jelly and she was certain that she swayed noticeably at Tyler's declaration. "I think I'd better sit down," she said weakly.

Tyler stared at her with concern. "Did I say something wrong?" His worried expression steadied Amy's legs.

"No," she managed to say, her voice so hoarse that it sounded nothing like normal. "You said something very right."

"I had hoped you felt the same way. I know we're moving things pretty fast, but I feel like we've lived a lifetime of experiences in the few short times we've spent together. After last night," Tyler sighed, "after last night, I knew. I knew without a doubt that I loved you."

He'd said it again. Amy felt a wash of excitement and wonder flood over her. "I still think I'd like to sit down," she whispered, and with a smile that lit up his eyes, Tyler assisted her back into the chair.

Amy was elated by Tyler's words, but in the back of her mind a nagging doubt crept in to spoil the perfect picture. Angie! Tyler immediately noticed the change in Amy and pulled up a chair to sit directly in front of her. "You might as well tell me what's on your mind, 'cause I'm not going away until you do."

Amy grimaced and nodded. "All right," she said with a sigh. "It's Angie. She fancies that you're the one man who can get her away from small town life. She's set her cap for you, I'm afraid, and a more determined force you will never have to reckon with."

Tyler rubbed his chin thoughtfully and shrugged his shoulders. "I'm honored that she thinks so highly of me, but it doesn't matter. She's a nice girl and I realize you look a great deal alike, some might even say identical, although I've noticed some differences. Anyway, Angie's not for me. I've no desire to live in the city. I've done that and it chokes the life out of me."

"But don't you see," Amy pleaded, "this thing will be between us. I love my sister and I don't want to hurt her. She'll think I worked against her, knowing what she had in mind for you, and that I stole you away from her. I can't have that kind of rivalry between us. I've fought too long and hard to avoid it."

"Is that why you don't have any other suitors?" Tyler asked softly.

"Yes, I suppose it is. The one man in this town who's paid me the slightest attention has only done so because his brothers forbid him to chase after Angie. You see, they both want her for themselves and refuse to have another rival for her attention." Amy couldn't believe she was sharing all of this with Tyler.

"I just don't want her hurt, Tyler," she stressed. "Angie's just being Angie and she really isn't trying to hurt me. She's just so used to me backing away from her conquests and leaving her to her designs."

"And what about this time?" Tyler asked with a raised brow. His face held a look of amusement that eased Amy's tension.

"This time, I'm not backing away," she replied in a whisper.

"Good," Tyler countered, "because I wouldn't let you if you tried." He reached out to hold her hand. "I can deal with Angie."

"How, without hurting her and making this an issue between sisters?"

"Leave it to me," he answered lightly. "I've had to deal with hundreds of mommas and their daughters. All who have set their strategies towards seeing me married. I've fought them off this long, I reckon I can handle one very lively Angela Carmichael."

Amy shook her head with a sadness in her eyes. "I don't think it will be that simple, Tyler. She's got a tender heart, in spite of her outward appearance of invincibility."

"Trust me, Amy. I will work this thing out so that it's Angie, herself, who loses interest. She'll cast me aside quick enough when she learns that I've no intention of living in the city or even moving close to one. When I make it clear that the open Kansas prairies are my home, she'll no doubt find a way to ease herself away from me."

Amy's face lit up. For the first time since this problem developed, she saw a way around having to battle with Angie for Tyler. "It just might work," she smiled.

"Trust me," Tyler said with a wink, "it'll work."

❧

Amy made herself scarce for the rest of the day so that Tyler would have time to speak with Angie. Because of the storm's relentless tirade, the entire family was trapped inside the house through the whole long day; Tyler would surely have plenty of opportunities to get his message across to Angie.

When supper time came, Amy joined her mother in the kitchen to help prepare the meal. Angie wandered in, seeming rather dejected, and Amy felt certain that Tyler had made his plans known to her.

"Angie, you can set the table while Amy cuts this bread," Dora said, noticing that Angie was just moving about aimlessly.

Angie did as she was told, setting the plates absent-mindedly on the red checkered tablecloth they used for everyday. Soon, Dora was calling the men to supper, and Amy found herself privileged to sit beside Tyler, while Angie quietly ate her dinner beside their mother. Apparently, Tyler's plan had worked.

＊

After supper, everyone gathered in the front parlor to talk and share stories of days gone by. Charles and Tyler shared a game of checkers, while Amy and Dora worked on quilt blocks. Angie excused herself to her room, much to everyone's surprise. Everyone except Amy, who knew that her sister had seen her dreams defeated in one swift blow. Her heart ached for her, and silently Amy prayed that God would send a man for Angie. One who would understand her needs and love her.

The wind died down around eight-thirty, and Amy found herself so tired that she too decided to excuse herself. Dora put aside her sewing and, with a nod to her husband, expressed her desire to also retire.

Charles stood and put a loving arm around his wife. "It's been a real joy having you here, Tyler. I'd like nothing better than if we could find a way to keep you on full-time as our parson. I intend to speak to the townsfolk and see if they aren't of the same mind. Do you suppose you might be interested in settling down in a tiny town like Deer Ridge?"

Tyler cast a quick glance at Amy and then smiled broadly at Charles and Dora. "I might be persuaded."

Charles laughed. "Somehow I thought you might be willing to consider it." With that, he and Dora went upstairs, leaving Amy and Tyler to follow.

Amy took one of the oil lamps and handed it to Tyler. "In case you want to read," she said and moved to extinguish the other lamps.

With nothing more than the soft glow from the fireplace and the lamp which Tyler held, Amy turned to study him for a moment. "Thank you," she finally said. "Thank you for caring and helping Angie through this."

Tyler moved forward and put an arm around Amy's shoulders. "I simply told her the truth," he answered. "I told her my heart could never be in the city."

Amy smiled knowingly and climbed the stairs with Tyler at her side. At the top, they stood for a moment before Tyler placed a brief kiss on Amy's mouth.

Amy felt a happiness like she'd never known, and her expression clearly revealed her heart. Without words, she went to her room, while Tyler moved in the opposite direction to the guest room.

"Thank You, God," she whispered against her closed bedroom door. She hugged her arms to her breasts and smiled, knowing that tonight's dreams would be the sweetest of all.

*

By morning the weather had cleared, leaving pale blue skies and sunshine against the snow white prairie fields. Huge drifts of snow had piled up against the house, barn, and fences. Anything that stood out as an obstacle to the blowing snow found itself insulated in white.

Tyler shared morning devotions with the Carmichaels before announcing his departure. Amy was happy to see that Angie was acting more like herself and smiled when her sister spoke of the Anderson brothers for the first time in weeks. Tyler was happy to see the recovery of Angie's lively spirit, as well. He'd felt confident that he could disinterest Angie in him as husband material, but like Amy, he was worried that she might somehow place the problem between her and her sister.

"When will you be back our way?" Charles asked, while Dora began clearing the breakfast dishes from the table.

"I plan to spend Christmas here," Tyler replied. "That is, if you think folks around here will approve."

Charles laughed. "I think they'll more than approve. It'll be our first Christmas with a real parson in charge. I'll see to it that plans get made for a real celebration. We'll have the kids put on a play or something and the ladies can all make those goodies we enjoy so much."

"I'll look forward to it then," Tyler said enthusiastically.

"Where are you headed after you leave here?" Dora asked. "I'd be happy to pack you some food for the road."

"I'd appreciate that, Dora. I promised to stop by the Riggs' place for the funeral. With this snow, I doubt many folks will be able to get away, and it will be difficult at best to make a proper grave. I want to offer Carl as much help as I can."

"Of course," Dora replied. "I don't imagine we'll be able to make the funeral." She glanced up to see her husband shake his head.

"I don't see how," Charles agreed. "I'm still not sure what kind of damage the storm has done. If we can, we'll go over later on and see what kind of help we can offer."

Amy remained silent throughout the exchange. She

hated the idea of Tyler leaving, and yet what else could he do? That was his job and if she were to marry him, it would be a big part of her life as well.

The thought of marriage to Tyler made Amy smile, and without her realizing, the attention of everyone in the room turned toward her.

"Looks like Amy's already a world away," Charles laughed.

Dora nudged her husband good-naturedly. "Now, leave her be, Pa. She's just day-dreamin'."

Amy blushed and lowered her head. No doubt they all knew full well what she was thinking about. Angie was the only one who seemed not to notice.

"Well, I for one will be glad when winter is over," Angie declared, moving to wash the dishes.

"Winter's just set in, Angie," her father mused. "You'd best just set your mind for a few more months of cold."

Tyler laughed and got to his feet. "I'd best get a move on."

Dora set about to make sandwiches for him to take along, while Amy packed some gingersnaps and sugar cookies. She was glad for some task to occupy her hands; otherwise, she feared she'd just sit and twist them until everyone knew she was upset and asked her why. Surprised by the flood of emotions that threatened to run out of control, she silently prayed that she'd not cry when Tyler departed.

When the moment did arrive, everyone bid Tyler farewell and managed to inconspicuously disappear, leaving Amy and Tyler alone.

"I'll miss you," Tyler said, pulling on his heavy coat. Amy nodded, afraid to speak. She lifted her eyes to his and saw the love shining clear. Mindless of proper manners, Amy threw herself into Tyler's arms and clung tightly to his broad frame.

"It won't be that long," Tyler whispered against her buried face. "And when I come back, I intend to ask you something quite important, so you'd best be ready to give me an answer."

Amy lifted her face to his and nodded. "I'll be ready," she replied. "I promise."

nine

Amy felt a giddy anticipation in the days that followed Tyler's departure. She missed him terribly, yet she felt as though she shared a private secret with him. Over and over, she remembered his words to her when they said goodbye, and she was certain that when he returned, he would ask her to marry him.

The snow kept them homebound for five days, but then a warm southerly breeze blew in and melted most of the drifts. Soon soggy brown puddles were all that remained. During the thaw, the twins' older brother Randy arrived to announce the birth of his new son.

"He's a big one, for sure," Randy boasted. "I measured him myself and he's pert near twenty-three inches long."

"My," Dora remarked in amazement. "He is good-sized."

"Congratulations, son." Charles gave Randy a hearty slap on his back. "How's Betsey doing?"

"She's fine. Tired, but fine. Doc was there this morning and said she needs to get plenty of rest. Other than that, he thinks both of them are good and strong."

"I'd be happy to come keep house and tend the children," Amy offered her brother.

"I was kind of hoping you might say that," Randy said with a smile. "I know it'd be a real peace of mind to Betsey. She doesn't trust me in her kitchen."

At this the family laughed. Even Angie teased him good-naturedly, "You must take after me."

"Naw," Randy teased right back, "nobody is as bad as

you are in the kitchen. At least I can make coffee."

Amy smiled, remembering the day Angie had filled the house with smoke when she had tried to impress Tyler with her culinary skills.

"He's got you on that one, Angie," Charles laughed. Then turning to Amy, he said, "You'd best get your things together."

Amy nodded and hurried upstairs. She was grateful for the job that awaited her, knowing that it would keep her mind occupied until Tyler returned.

She calculated the days left until his return, and then she smiled again. Maybe she'd even be married before the year was out! The idea warmed her like a toasty quilt. She hugged her arms around herself, imagining what Tyler would say when he saw her again, and then she laughed out loud at herself when she realized what she was doing.

"I'm always telling folks to take one day at a time—but ever since Tyler's come into my life, it's all I can do to keep from dreaming away my days," she said aloud. "Maybe Tyler was right. Maybe I found it easy to keep from planning beyond today, because I had no one to plan for or with."

She threw the things she would need at Randy's house into a a worn carpet bag. Then she headed downstairs to join her brother. She determined in her mind to take life one day at a time, just as she always had before she met Tyler, but her heart was already rebelling at the idea.

&

In the weeks that followed, Amy found that caring for Betsey and the baby was the easy part of her responsibilities. The hard part was keeping Charlie, Petey, and Dolly amused. Blustery winter weather confined them to the house, and out of boredom, they insisted on constant attention.

Amy tried to fuss over each one of them. She took great joy in getting to know the newest Carmichael, baby Joseph whom everyone already called Joey, but she tried to remember that the needs of the other children were just as important as the baby's. Dolly, used to being the youngest, had her nose slightly out of joint when it came to sharing attention with her baby brother. She didn't want to give up without a fight the important job of being the family baby.

Amy soothed her niece by telling her it would be far more fun to help with Joey, than to cry over the attention he got. Dolly was a bit young to understand logical reasoning, but Amy found a sugar cookie usually helped matters greatly.

Petey and Charlie were intrigued with the ruddy faced bundle, but the attraction wore off quickly. Soon they were begging to bundle up and go outside, and then they tracked in mud and snow from their outdoor adventures.

Before long, Betsey was up and around, and the need for Amy to stay lessened with each passing day. Finally, when Christmas was only a week away, Amy bid them goodbye and headed home.

"Only a week," she told the horse on their journey to the Carmichael farm. "Only one more week and Tyler will be back."

The horse flicked his ears and plodded faithfully along the soggy prairie. Amy gazed out across the fields and sighed. The land was so open here, so vast and empty, yet life was only asleep; Amy knew when spring arrived the prairie would come to life once again.

Even the gray skies overhead could not dampen her spirits, and Amy found herself humming a tune. She loved thinking about a life with Tyler. She wondered where they would live and whether she would travel with her husband on his circuit. Most circuit riders rode alone, she thought, and frowned at the lengthy separations their wives must know.

Maybe Pa will talk the town folks into giving Tyler a job right here, she thought. Especially if we're married. The idea pacified her concerns, and Amy's thoughts turned to what she'd do once she arrived home.

❧

She rode into the yard just before noon and found an animated Angie awaiting her. They walked together to the barn, but when Amy prepared to unsaddle her horse, Angie reached out to stop her.

"I was hoping you'd ride into town with me," Angie said. "I haven't done much Christmas shopping, and now there's only a few days left."

Amy froze, realizing that she'd not prepared anything for Tyler in the way of a Christmas gift. What should she do for him? Should she make something or purchase some trinket at Smith's General Store? Her mind raced with ideas, totally blocking out Angie's ramblings.

"You aren't listening to me!" Angie exclaimed at last.

Amy stroked the horse's mane and sighed. "Sorry, Angie. I was just thinking about what you'd said. I managed to make something for Ma before I left, but I don't have a thing for Pa or you." She carefully didn't bring Tyler into the conversation.

"Then you'll go with me?" Angie asked hopefully.

"Sure." Amy smiled. "Let me get my money and a bite to eat, and I'll be ready."

Angie flew into the house to tell their mother what the girls had planned. Angie even made a sandwich for Amy in order to hurry things along.

❧

The girls rode side by side, saying little until they neared the small town of Deer Ridge. To call it a town seemed a bit of a boast, but it was all they had and Amy loved it. The handful of buildings made up what folks affectionately called "Main Street". On one side stood the general store and bank, along with several smaller establishments, including the barber shop and Doc Taggert's place. On the opposite side of the street was Nathan Gallagher's law office, the livery stables and blacksmith's shop, and further down from this was the new school building. Opposite the school building at the other end of town was the hotel/boarding house.

Smith's General Store was the main attraction for the small community, however. Folks gathered here to discuss the weather and crops, new babies and deaths, and whatever else came to mind. Socializing wasn't an every day occurrence, it was a luxury, and if one had to make the trip into town, he or she had the responsibility of bringing back all the news that bore repeating.

Tying their horses to the hitching post, Amy and Angie pulled their coats closer as a blast of frigid prairie wind pushed them along. "Pa says it's going to snow tonight for sure," Angie said with a shiver.

"He's usually right about those things," Amy replied and added, "so we'd best get to it and get back home."

Angie paused for a moment outside the clapboard storefront. "Uh, Amy," she said hesitantly.

Amy turned and eyed her sister suspiciously. "What are you up to, Angie?"

"Nothing," Angie hedged, "it's just that I saw Nathan go into his office across the way and I thought, I mean. . ."

"Go on and see him." Amy shook her head. "You and I neither one will enjoy this trip if you don't attend to all of your beaus. I'm sure Ed Anderson will be slighted if you don't make the rounds to the bank as well."

Angie laughed and gave her head a toss. "I don't care if he is. He hasn't been to see me in over a week."

"And Nathan has?" Amy teased.

"Well, no," Angie admitted. "But Nathan's practice keeps him busy."

Amy had to laugh at the idea of an abundance of law work in Deer Ridge. "The idea of a rail road spur coming this way is the only thing that keeps Nathan Gallagher busy. Tell them all hello for me," Amy replied. She left Angie contemplating her words.

᪐

Inside the store, the pot belly stove was nearly glowing red from the hearty fire that Jeremy Smith had built to keep his customers warm. Several of the community's prominent members stood discussing important matters when Amy entered. The gentlemen tipped their hats, and the only other woman, Mrs. Smith, came quickly to Amy's side.

"Land sakes, child, whatever are you doing out on a day like this? Come get warmed up." The gray-headed woman pushed her way through the men, dragging Amy with her to the stove.

"Angie and I needed to do a bit of last minute shopping. You know," Amy whispered in the woman's ear, "for Christmas."

Betty Smith nodded and shared the excitement of the moment with Amy. "Who are you still shopping for?"

"Pa and Angie," she said right away, and then with a quick glance around her to make certain no one could overhear, she added, "and the new pastor."

Betty smiled, revealing two missing teeth. "I heard tell he'd spent a deal of time out your way. Is there something I should know about you and him?"

Amy blushed and lowered her head. "No, but when there is, I'll let you know."

"Why, Amy Carmichael!" the woman exclaimed a bit louder than she'd intended. Ears around them perked up, so Betty pulled Amy away from the crowd and toward the back of the store. "I'll bet your ma's plumb tickled pink. She's always a frettin' that you'd never find anyone to settle down with."

Amy felt her face grow even more flushed. Did everybody have to know her business? Seeing her discomfort, Betty began showing Amy some of the trinkets they'd stocked with Christmas in mind.

"That silver mirror is pretty," Amy said and immediately thought of Angie's love of primping. "I'd imagine my sister would like that very much."

"Where is Angie?" Betty asked, setting the mirror aside.

"Oh, you know Angie. She had to make the rounds."

Betty laughed, because she did know Angie and her love of flirting with half the town.

Amy continued to shop for the next half hour or so before finally settling on the mirror for Angie and a brass handled jackknife for her father. Buying a gift for Tyler proved to be an easy task when Amy spied the newest collection of books. Tyler had mentioned his love of reading, and with this in mind, Amy quickly sorted through the stack and picked out Dickens' *A Tale of Two Cities*.

Thumbing through the book, Amy remembered her father telling about a series of public readings which Charles Dickens had performed in America. The man had taken the country by storm, and his works were quite popular.

Tucking the book under her arm, Amy glanced around to see if Angie had returned. Most of the other customers had filtered out, and now, with the exception of the self-appointed Mayor Osborne, who was in a heated argument with Jeremy Smith, the store was empty.

"Betty?" Amy called into the back room where she'd seen Betty take her other purchases.

The woman emerged with two brightly wrapped packages. "I thought this might dress them up a bit," she said proudly. "And don't be fretting that I'll charge you, 'cause I won't. I just happened to have it left over from my own things."

"Oh, Betty, it's wonderful. Thank you!" Amy held out Tyler's book. "I'm going to take this as well. I'd be happy to pay for it to be wrapped."

"This for the pastor?" Betty asked with a grin. Amy nodded and waited while the woman disappeared into the back to wrap the book.

When she'd paid for her things and Angie still had not appeared, Amy could do nothing but try and find her sister. She tucked her gifts into one of the saddle bags, then made her way across the street to Nathan Gallagher's office.

Opening the door to the law office, Amy peeked in. No one was in the outer room, and she saw no sign that Angie had ever been there. Amy started to step out when she heard voices coming from the other room. Thinking that Nathan and Angie were talking in his office, Amy quietly moved to the door and started to knock.

Her hand was nearly against the wood when she heard Nathan's voice bellow, "I don't care what you think! We'll take the bank money on Christmas morning when that fool of a pastor is teaching the town about charity and love."

Amy's heart pounder harder, and she froze in place. Her hand was still lifted to knock, but for some reason she couldn't bring herself to move.

"Gallagher, you're a hard man," a voice commented. "I guess I'll take my share and be on my way. You can do this job on your own."

"Have it your way, but go out the back door. I don't want anyone seeing you." Nathan's voice was clearly agitated. "Oh, and here." Amy heard a clinking thud as something hit the floor. "Don't forget your money."

The other man grumbled, and then she heard the sound of a door being opened and closed. Amy hadn't been able to bring herself to move, but she suddenly realized what a precarious position she'd placed herself in. She backed away slowly from the closed door.

She'd made it halfway to the front door, when she stumbled into a spittoon and sent it crashing over with a resounding clang. Nathan was through the door in a heartbeat, staring dumbfounded at Amy. He tried to decide for a moment whether she was coming or going, but Amy didn't give him any time to figure it out before she turned to run for the door.

He was on her before she'd taken two steps, gripping her wrist with his steely hand and dragging her back to his office for privacy.

"What are you doing here, Angie?" he asked, mistaking her for her sister.

"I, I . . ." Amy tried to speak but the words wouldn't come.

"What did you hear?" Nathan shoved her into a chair.

Amy shook her head. "Nothing. I came here to find my sister."

"What would Amy be doing here?" Nathan frowned and then his eyes narrowed. "You're not Angie." His words seemed to hang forever on the air.

"Yes," Amy finally admitted. "Angie and I were shopping and she said she was coming to visit you. I was just trying to find her so that we could go home." Amy timidly came up from the chair, only to have Nathan whirl around and slam her back down.

"Stay there!"

Amy trembled, but she did as she was told, while Nathan moved quickly to lock his office door. She cast a quick glance toward the back door, knowing if she could somehow make it there, she'd be safe.

Nathan came back to where she sat, putting himself between her and freedom. He rubbed his jaw for a moment and stared at her, his hard eyes boring into her face. "You know, don't you?"

Amy tried to look innocent and shook her head. "Know what?"

"Don't play games with me, Amy. You aren't going to ruin my plans. I can't have you out there bringing the town down on me. You overheard my plans or you wouldn't be so afraid of me."

"I'm wasn't afraid until you grabbed me and dragged me in here," Amy said angrily. "I don't know why you're treating me like this, but when my Pa and brother find out, you won't have time to worry about any plans you've made." She prayed he'd be convinced that she hadn't overheard his conversation with the now absent stranger.

Nathan moved away from her, thinking. As a lawyer, part of his job was to study men and what they had to say, determining whether or not they were telling the truth. He had to admit, Amy Carmichael was either a very good actress or she truly hadn't overhead his plans. Still, if she hadn't heard him talking, why was she running from him?

When Nathan turned his back to retrieve a drink he'd poured earlier, Amy bolted for the back door. She had managed to get it open before Nathan slammed her against it.

"I won't say anything!" Amy exclaimed without thinking. Nathan was twisting her arm behind her so violently that she thought she'd pass out from the pain.

"I thought you didn't know anything," Nathan sneered. "How can you say anything about something you didn't hear?"

Amy knew he'd caught her and she hung her head in dejection. "What are you going to do with me?"

"That, my dear, does present a problem," Nathan said, pulling her back to the chair. "I have no desire to kill anyone over a matter of a mere several thousand dollars. Still," he paused to push her into the seat, "I won't have you mess this up for me."

Amy said nothing, waiting and watching while Nathan contemplated her fate. "I suppose," he continued, "if I can keep you out of the way until after the job is done, I won't have to kill you."

Amy blanched at his statement, making Nathan laugh. "Don't worry, little Amy. You just cooperate with me and I'll figure this out. Otherwise—well, let's just say, it won't be a Merry Christmas at the Carmichaels'."

ten

Amy struggled against the ropes that bound her hands and feet. She tried to yell, but the gag Nathan had placed firmly over her mouth muted any sound that came from her throat.

Quieting for a moment, Amy listened to hear if Nathan was still in the building. He had dumped her in the storage closet with orders to keep quiet or else. When he told her he had to get her horse out of sight, Amy knew he meant business; she could hardly believe this was the same man who had courted Angie. "Please," she had tried to say through the gag, but Nathan locked the closet door and left her alone in the darkness.

He had tied her hands tightly behind her back so she would have no chance of freeing herself. Nevertheless, Amy worked at the ropes until her wrists were chafed and sore. She felt her eyes fill with tears, but she refused to give in to her misery. Somehow, she had to get out of this.

ఈ

Angie finally made her entrance into Smith's General Store, only to find Amy already gone. Betty assured her that Amy had gone in search of Angie when her shopping was completed, so Angie took the time necessary to finish her own Christmas shopping, certain that Amy would return any minute. When she didn't, Angie started to get worried. After paying for her things, Angie went outside and looked up and down the street.

The sun was already well to the west, and Angie knew they'd stayed a great deal longer than they should have. Noticing Ed Anderson as he came out to lock up the bank, Angie ran toward him.

"Ed, have you seen Amy?" she asked breathlessly.

"Angie!" Ed grinned. "Why didn't you tell me you were coming to town?"

"Didn't know myself until just today," Angie replied. "I'm looking for Amy. She rode in with me to do some shopping, but now I can't find her."

Ed laughed. "Deer Ridge isn't that big. She must be around here somewhere. Did you check over at the post office—or maybe Miller's Hotel? You know how Mrs. Miller likes to visit."

"You mean gossip—and no, I hadn't checked there." Angie smoothed her hair and smiled up at Ed, but her lips were still tight with worry. "I was visiting with Mrs. Miller earlier, myself. Maybe Amy and I just crossed paths."

"That's probably it," Ed agreed. "Would you like me to walk with you over to the Hotel?"

The worry eased from Angie's face. Ever the flirt, she batted her eyes and extended her arm. "I would simply love it!"

Passing by the store again on their way down Main Street, Ed noticed the solitary horse that stood outside. "You girls didn't ride double, did you?"

"What are you talking about, Ed?"

Ed pointed toward Angie's horse. "You said you rode in together. Did Amy ride her own horse?"

"Yes, yes, she did," Angie replied. She shrugged her shoulders. "Maybe she was mad at me for taking so long and she got tired of waiting for me. I'll bet she rode on home without me. That would figure."

"Sure would." Ed laughed. "I guess the joke's on you for taking too much time visiting around the town."

Confident that this was true, Angie allowed Ed to help her up onto her horse. "She's probably already home sitting safe and warm in front of the fireplace."

"If you give me a minute," Ed said, "I'll go saddle up my horse and ride part of the way home with you. I promised Ma I'd bring out some supplies tonight for her baking, so I've got to go that way anyway."

Angie's face lit up, and her frustration with Amy disappeared. "I'll wait right here for you."

❧

Dark had nearly fallen by the time Angie finally rode into the farmyard. She'd had the most wonderful time with Ed, and she was still wearing her dreamy expression when her father met her in the barn.

"I was beginning to get worried," Charles said, helping her from the saddle.

"I'm sorry, Pa. I took time to try and find Amy, and before I knew it, the sun was sinking lower and lower. Ed Anderson rode out as far as the creek with me, so I didn't have far to come alone."

"Alone?" Charles frowned. "Where's your sister?"

Angie's mouth dropped open. "You mean she's not here?"

"No." Charles's voice was flat. "What made you think she was?"

"We separated in town because I went to see Mrs. Miller at the Hotel. She'd promised to make me some lace as a Christmas present for Amy. I stayed too long I guess, 'cause when I headed back to the store, Amy was already gone. I went to look for her after I finished my shopping, but I couldn't find her anywhere." Angie twisted a curl around her finger nervously. "I saw Ed Anderson locking up the bank, so I went and asked him if he'd seen Amy. He hadn't, but he offered to look for her with me. That was when we noticed her horse was gone."

"Amy's horse was gone?" A frown lined Charles's normally cheerful face.

Angie nodded. "We figured she'd gotten mad at me for taking so long and had headed home on her own. That's why I came on home myself. I thought she'd be here."

Charles was already pulling the saddle off Angie's horse. "You give this horse some feed and water. I'm going back in town to look for your sister. Tell your ma what happened, but try not to tell it so as she worries too much. Amy's probably still looking for you, so there ain't no reason to get her frettin'."

Angie nodded. She was starting to feel anxious for her twin. Amy was not the type to act irresponsibly, Angie realized, and she should have known Amy would never have gotten mad and left her. Angie quickly cared for the horse and hurried inside to tell her mother what had happened.

ꙮ

Amy knew it was only a matter of time before Nathan returned. She pondered what he might do with her in order to keep her from spilling his plans. She still couldn't fully comprehend that the handsome, young lawyer planned to rob the town of its harvest money.

Without even realizing what she was doing, Amy began to pray. Lord, she thought, I need help out of this one, for sure. Please send someone to rescue me. And keep me from the harm Nathan Gallagher plans for me. Please, she added, help me not to be afraid. It was only a brief prayer, but it strengthened her spirits, and Amy began to have hope that she would somehow escape.

Waiting there in the dark, her mind turned to thoughts of Tyler. He would be arriving any day now, and Amy wondered if he would be the one to find her. She fell into a daydream where Tyler rode up to Nathan's office and pulled her out of the closet, into his strong arms. How terribly romantic, she thought, and had to laugh at her nonsense.

She'd no doubt be home long before Tyler returned. But thinking about that was just as romantic, for then he'd ask her to marry him, and she would of course say yes. She fell deep into another daydream.

The sound of someone entering the law office caught her attention. She began to pound her feet against the floor and threw her shoulder against the wall of the closet. The door to the closet swung open, and light from a lantern blinded Amy's eyes for a moment. "Quiet down—or else," Nathan whispered harshly.

Amy sat still while her eyes adjusted to the light. Nathan placed the lamp on the floor and began searching his pockets for something.

"I've decided to take you out of here," he said while pulling a handkerchief from his pocket. "I have a problem, though. I can't very well parade you down Main Street, now can I?"

He laughed at Amy's expressin and continued. "I paid a visit to Doc Taggert. Well, actually to his office. You might say I allowed myself entrance through the back window in order to retrieve this." He held up a corked bottle of liquid.

Amy shied away, trying to scoot back against the closet wall. She was only too certain of what Nathan had in mind. He uncorked the bottle and poured a liberal amount of the contents onto his handkerchief before continuing. "This way, it will be a lot easier on me and you both."

Amy shook her head furiously. She kicked at Nathan when he moved closer to her. Her strangled protests couldn't make it past the gag, but Nathan understood their meaning well enough.

"Don't fight me, Amy. I can't let you spoil this for me. I've worked too hard and too long on this. You're a good girl and I don't want to hurt you. Now just cooperate with me and it'll all be over in a short time."

Amy felt a scream rise up inside her, only to die as Nathan pulled her forward. He held the cloth firmly against her face, and in spite of her thrashing from side to side, the chloroform did its job. Amy had a burning sensation in her nostrils and throat, and then the darkness overtook her.

☙

She came awake slowly, almost like she'd been a part of some strange dream. She lifted her aching head and tried to focus on the images around her, but nothing made sense. Dropping her head back, she waited for a few moments, hoping her head would clear before she tried to lift it again.

Her lips felt sore and dry, and she ran her tongue across them. She remembered the gag then—it was gone! With that memory, everything else came back to her. She was lying on a bed somewhere, and she swung her legs over the side, realizing that the ropes had been cut from her hands and feet. She sat up, her head swimming.

Her head pounded with the echo of each beat of her heart, and her throat was scratchy and sore from the chloroform. When she could finally focus a bit better, she noticed a small table across the room from the bed. On it, a lantern offered the room's only light.

Amy got to her feet slowly, testing her weight against her wobbly legs. When she felt confident she could stand, she walked to the table and inspected the items on top of it. Nathan had left her a jar of water, a loaf of bread, and the light.

Looking around the room, Amy surmised that it must be a dugout or root cellar. She climbed the two dirt steps that led to a wooden door and pulled at the handle to open it. It wouldn't budge—but then she really hadn't expected it to. Heaving a sigh, she stepped away and took a more careful inventory of the room's contents.

There was the makeshift bed she'd been lying on, the table, and nothing else. Overhead was the dirt and grass ceiling that was typical of dugouts, but with no stove and no hole in the roof for a flue, Amy decided this must be someone's deserted storage cellar.

She returned her gaze to the table, then again to the door, and at last sat back down on the bed. She was trapped without hope, and the silence of her prison broke her like nothing else could have. She lay back on the bed and began to sob.

eleven

Charles Carmichael pounded on the door to the general store. After several moments, Jeremy Smith's scowling face appeared in the window.

"You know we're closed," he called from behind the glass.

Charles was undaunted. "Jeremy, have you seen Amy?" he bellowed.

His expression erased Jeremy's scowl. He opened the door and shook his head. "Not since earlier when she was shopping."

The lines in Charles's face grew deeper. "She's missing," he said heavily. "I've looked all over for her. I covered the miles between here and home as best I could, but I didn't see any sign of her anywhere. I was hoping she'd be somewhere still in town."

"I'll get my coat and a light," Jeremy said. He knew no one would be able to rest until the young woman was found.

"I'm going to ride out to the Anderson place," Charles said. "If they haven't seen anything of her, then I'll bring George and his boys back with me to help with the search. Would you get the men together here and wait for us?"

"Sure thing, Charles. We'll be waitin' for you right here."

Confident that Jeremy would help, Charles mounted his horse and rode as fast as he dared to the Anderson farm. Snow was beginning to fall as he dismounted, but Charles barely noticed. He charged toward the house, ignoring the barking dogs, but the commotion brought George Anderson to the door before Charles could knock.

"Charles!" George exclaimed. "What are you doing out here on a night like this? A guy would have to be pert near crazy to brave the winds tonight."

"You haven't seen Amy, have you, George." Charles's words were a statement rather than a question. He wiped the snow flakes from his face, and took a deep breath. "She went into town with Angie and never came home."

By this time Ed and Jack had joined their father at the door. "I thought she'd ridden out ahead of Angie," Ed said. "I helped Angie look for her until we noticed her horse was gone. We figured she'd gone home."

"If she headed toward home," Charles said, fear making his voice gruff, "she never made it. I've got Jeremy Smith getting the men together in town. I wanted to ask. . ."

"No need to ask, Charles," George interrupted. "Boys, get your brother and tell your ma what's happened."

Ed and Jack quickly returned with Jacob, closely followed by Emma Anderson. "Is there anything I can do, Charles?" Emma asked.

"Pray," Charles suggested. "Just pray for her safe return. I know your prayers will be joined by an awful lot of others petitionin' God for the same thing. I just have to believe that Amy will be safe in our Father's hands."

"I know she is," Emma said firmly. "And I'll be praying for both her and for you men as you search." She reached out to squeeze Charles's hand, then watched as her family prepared to leave with Charles.

"Bar the door, Emma," her husband told her as they left. "We don't know what's amiss and there's no sense taking chances." He kissed her lightly on the cheek, picked up his rifle, and followed his sons outside.

Alone in the cold, damp room, Amy shivered and hugged her arms around herself. She was grateful she still wore her heavy coat, but she was still cold. She pulled the thin bed blanket around her to add to her coat's warmth and tried to breathe slowly and calmly. She could do nothing now but wait. Surely Nathan wouldn't just leave her here to die; after all, he had provided food and water for her.

She got off the bed and paced back and forth across the room, trying to warm herself by moving around. Her thoughts turned to home, and she bit her lip while her eyes burned with tears. Her parents would be frantic, and Angie would blame herself. Amy breathed a silent prayer that God would ease their worry, and she asked again for a speedy rescue.

She tried to focus on pleasant thoughts and not give into the fear and hopelessness of her situation. She was uncertain how long she had been unconcious, and she wondered what day it was. Days might have already passed, she told herself, and rescue could be very near. Clinging to that hope, she ate a small piece of the bread, allowing herself no more than a brief swallow of the water. She knew rationing could be essential, because she had no guarantee that Nathan would return to supply her with more.

As the hours dragged by, she spent most of her time praying and remembering. The air grew colder, and she feared she might freeze to death before anyone could find her. She felt more and more sleepy, but she knew sleeping could be dangerous in the cold, and so she forced herself to stay awake by reciting Bible verses and signing hymns.

"Father," she said aloud. Even the sound of her own

voice was welcome in the silence. "I need a miracle. I don't know what's happening out there or even where I am, but You know, and I know You're watching over me. Please let them find me in time, Lord—and if not, then teach me how I can help myself get out of this." She didn't add a closing "amen," for she knew her prayer would continue again when the stillness became too much for her once more.

&

Tyler approached the Carmichael farm with the giddy excitement of a schoolboy. He'd arranged to have three weeks away from his circuit, while another rider took his place during his absence. During those three weeks, he intended to make plans with Amy for their wedding.

Snow covered the ground now, and Tyler was reminded of the storm that had kept him at the Carmichaels' long enough to share his true feelings with Amy. He smiled to himself, thinking of how worried she'd been about her sister's feelings. That was one of the things he loved most about Amy. She was always looking out for the folks around her before ever considering her own needs.

Without stopping at the house first, Tyler went directly to the barn. He cared for his horse and then ran across the yard to the house. Slightly breathless, he knocked on the door. A red-eyed Dora opened it.

"Tyler!" she gasped in surprise. Her face twisted with emotions that Tyler could not identify, and then she turned to her husband. "Look, Charles, it's Tyler."

The skin on the back of Tyler's neck prickled when he saw how haggard both of Amy's parents were. They ushered him into the kitchen without a word and motioned him toward a seat. When Dora and Charles had sat down with him, he leaned toward them, waiting for them to speak.

"What is it?" he asked finally. He knew in his heart he wasn't going to like the answer. "Has something happened to Amy?"

Dora began to cry anew, and Charles put his face in his hands. "She's gone," he said. The sorrow in his muffled words made Tyler believe she was dead.

"Dear God," he breathed, feeling his own heart break. "What happened? How did she. . .?" He fell silent, unable to utter the word.

Dora instantly realized what he was thinking. "She's not dead, Tyler! At least we pray to God she's not."

Relief washed over him, but the sick feeling that filled his stomach refused to leave. "Then what are you saying?"

Charles leaned back in his chair and shook his head. "She's been missing ever since she went into town with Angie. They went Christmas shopping four, no, five days ago, and Amy hasn't been seen since."

Tyler's heart pounded in his ears, nearly drowning the words Charles spoke. "We got a search party together," Charles continued, "but there wasn't a clue anywhere. It was like she simply disappeared off the face of the earth."

"Is anybody else missing?" Tyler asked.

"No," Charles replied. "Everyone else is accounted for. None of her friends have seen her. Even her horse has disappeared."

"Her horse?"

Charles nodded. "She and Angie both rode horseback into town. When Angie saw that Amy's horse was missing, she presumed she'd ridden home without her. Angie's beside herself. She blames herself for not sticking around and waiting."

Dora sighed. "I've tried to talk to her, but she won't

even open her door."

ↀ

Angie tossed fitfully in her bed. She'd tried to sleep, but whenever she closed her eyes a cold foreboding settled upon her and she felt a misery that she'd never known. People often said twins were bonded to one another, and although she had never experienced it before, Angie couldn't help but wonder if what she was feeling now was actually the echo of Amy's suffering.

The knock at her bedroom door brought her upright in the bed. "Leave me be, Ma," Angie called in a ragged voice.

"Angie, it's Tyler. Please open the door and talk to me."

Angie swallowed hard and felt a trembling start at her head and go clear to her toes. Her mother had already told her how much Amy cared for Tyler. She'd also told Angie that she was quite confident Tyler cared deeply for Amy. Angie couldn't help but believe Tyler would blame her for Amy's disappearance. "And why shouldn't he?" Angie muttered to herself.

"Angie," Tyler persisted. "Please open the door. It's not your fault that Amy is gone—but you may be the only one who can really help us find her."

At these words Angie jumped to her feet and threw open her door. "How?" She stared into Tyler's face. "How can I possibly help her?"

Tyler studied the young woman before him. She was the image of his Amy, but in some ways she was different as well. The differences were especially clear now after the days of worry and grief Angie had spent alone. She had dark circles under her eyes, and her face was gaunt and pale.

Tyler put his arm around Angie's shoulders. "Come

downstairs and let's talk."

Angie nodded and allowed him to lead the way. When she saw her parents waiting in the kitchen, she nearly turned to run back to her room, but Tyler's grip was firm.

They looked so old, Angie thought, taking the chair Tyler pulled out for her. Did they hate her for doing this to them? Would they ever forgive her for leaving Amy? Angie buried her face in her hands and sobbed.

"I should have never left her. This is all my fault and you all hate me now."

Dora looked at her in stunned silence, while Charles nearly dropped the cup of coffee he'd been nursing.

"Nobody blames you, Angie," Tyler said. "Nobody except yourself."

Angie looked up at him with tear-filled eyes. "I feel like Cain in the Bible," she cried. "I was my sister's keeper and now. . ." She couldn't say any more and put her head on the table to cry.

Tyler put his arm around her. "Father," he prayed, "please comfort Angie in her pain. She feels responsible for her sister, but we know that isn't the case. Help her, Lord, to see that her parents love her a great deal and that no one holds her accountable for Amy's disappearance. Father, guide us to Amy and show us the way to bring her home. In Jesus' name, amen."

Angie's tears slowed, and finally she leaned back in her chair and sighed. Her father reached out and covered her hand with his own. Taking in another deep, ragged breath, she steadied her nerves. "What do you want to know?" She lifted her face to Tyler's imploring eyes.

"Just start from the beginning and tell me everything," he said with a smile of hope. "Don't leave out anything, no matter how insignificant it might seem."

ra

Some time later, Tyler rode into Deer Ridge. He wouldn't rest until he'd questioned people himself, and so he made his way to where several of the townspeople stood talking in a cluster in front of the store.

"Howdy, folks." He climbed down from his horse. "I heard about Amy and was hoping to help locate her." He wasted no time with formalities.

"I think Injuns took her," the hotel owner, Mrs. Miller, stated firmly.

Cora Peterson scoffed at this. "Tweren't no Injuns, Bertha. Don't you ever think Injuns got better things to do than snatch up white folks? Might as well blame the Swedes."

"Well, it could of happened," Bertha Miller sniffed. "It hasn't been that long since Little Big Horn. They might be feeling riled at white folk, and Amy might just have been in the wrong place at the wrong time."

At this Cora's husband Bud stepped in and waved the woman away. "Don't get her started on Little Big Horn or we'll never get to hear what the preacher has to say."

The crowd smiled, in spite of their worry, and even Bertha seemed to relax a bit. Tyler was grateful for the break in the tension he'd known since first learning of Amy's disappearance.

He talked with the folks for a few more minutes before heading into the general store. At the sound of the front door being opened, Jeremy Smith came from the back room. For once the store was strangely void of activity. Maybe, thought Tyler, people are too tense to relax inside the store the way they would normally.

"Good to see you, Parson," Jeremy Smith said, extending a hand over the counter.

"It's good to be back, although, I had hoped for more pleasant circumstances," Tyler replied.

Betty Smith joined her husband, fear clearly etched in the weathered lines of her face. "Pastor Andrews." She greeted him with a nod.

"I'm glad we're alone," Tyler said, glancing around him. "I hoped you could give me the details about the day Amy disappeared. I promised her folks I'd help look for her."

Betty's eyes misted with tears. "You know, she bought you a Christmas present." The words were out before she realized it. "I'm sorry, I shouldn't have spoiled the surprise, but. . ."

"It's all right, Mrs. Smith." Tyler smiled. "I know Amy would understand and I promise to be surprised." Tyler was deeply touched to think that Amy's thoughts had been on him.

He stayed long enough to listen to the Smiths tell every detail they could remember. When the couple fell silent, Tyler mulled the information over for a moment and then asked one final question.

"You say she was going to look for Angie when she left here. Where might she have thought to find her?"

"My guess," Mrs. Smith answered, "would be that Amy figured she was visiting her beaus. Ed Anderson would have been over at the bank and Nathan Gallagher's office is across the street."

Her husband nodded in agreement, and Tyler took a deep breath. At least he had a place to start.

twelve

Talking to Ed Anderson revealed nothing more than Tyler already knew. Ed went over every detail patiently, even though he'd already told his story a dozen or more times to the Carmichael men. He understood Tyler's anxiety because Charles had told him in confidence that Amy and Tyler had feelings for one another. Ed tried to offer Tyler comfort, and he promised he'd continue to search for Amy as his time allowed.

Tyler picked up his hat and coat and headed for the door.

"You know, Tyler," Ed said, returning to his desk, "Nathan Gallagher has been pretty quiet about this whole thing. You might want to see if he knows any more than I do. If he'll talk to you."

"I was headed over there now," Tyler said. "I'll stress the need for his cooperation."

Ed smiled at the towering pastor's back. No doubt he would get his point across to Mr. Gallagher.

Tyler let himself in the law office and tossed his hat and coat on the nearest chair. "Hello!" he called.

Nathan Gallagher came from his office with a look of surprise. "You're the circuit rider, aren't you?" He looked Tyler up and down.

"That's right," Tyler responded. "I'm also a good friend of the Carmichaels. I'm trying to help them locate their daughter."

Nathan stiffened slightly. "I see. And just what has that

to do with me? I've already told Mr. Carmichael I know nothing about Amy's whereabouts."

Tyler was taken aback by the man's cool manner. Everyone else had greeted him with somber cooperation and earnest concern, but Nathan Gallagher seemed not only indifferent to Amy's plight but almost angry at the interruption.

"Folks tell me that Amy was last seen looking for her sister," Tyler said. "Everybody knows that Angie has a number of gentlemen callers, one of which is you. I figured it might be possible that Angie came to see you the day Amy disappeared—and that Amy might have come by here looking for her." Tyler leaned against the wall in a casual manner, making it clear to Nathan Gallagher that he intended to stay until he got some answers.

"It's true that I've called on Angie before," Nathan acknowledged. "But Angie didn't come to see me that day. Amy wouldn't have any reason to come here without Angie."

"She would if she were looking for her sister," Tyler said. "That would be a logical thing to do, now, wouldn't it?" His eyes were intense, watching Gallagher's reaction.

If the lawyer thought he was good at reading people's expressions, then Tyler Andrews was a genius at it. He noticed the way Nathan's eyes darted from side to side to avoid his own, and he saw the way Nathan's hands fidgeted in his pockets.

Nathan shrugged, feigning nonchalance. "I guess that's reasonable, but Amy didn't come here. I told her father that and now I'm telling you."

"I'm just trying to find her," Tyler said calmly. Inside, however, he was boiling at Nathan's lack of concern.

"Well, I believe you've done all you can here," the lawyer said firmly. "Now if you'll excuse me, I have work to do."

Tyler allowed him to return to his office without another word. Something told him that Gallagher knew more than he was saying, but Tyler could not force him to reveal what he knew. Frustrated, Tyler pulled on his coat and hat and retrieved his horse from the front of the general store. Then he turned toward the Carmichael farm, eager to see if Randy or Charles had learned anything more.

When at last Tyler arrived back at the farm, he felt more discouraged than he'd ever felt in his life. Amy was out there somewhere, maybe hurt, definitely scared, and he couldn't help her. He wanted so much to let her know that he cared, that he would always care, but he had no leads, no answers to the questions that could help him find her.

When he approached the house, his heart jumped. Amy's horse was tied out front along side another that he didn't recognize. Had she been found? God surely must have heard his prayers. He nearly flew off his horse and into the house.

"That's Amy's horse!" He pushed into the kitchen without so much as a knock.

Randy Carmichael stood against the stove warming his hands. "I found it in Hays," he said without looking up. "The livery owner said a man came in several days ago and sold it to him, tack and all, for twenty dollars."

"Did he get a description of the man?" Tyler asked.

"He did," Charles said, coming in from the other room. He nodded down the hall. "Dora and Angie are pretty upset by this. I told them to leave the discussion to us."

Tyler nodded. "It's probably best." He turned to Randy

and asked again about the man.

"Livery said the man was about six foot tall," Randy answered. "Heavy set, scraggly red beard, and hair down to his shoulders. He wasn't dressed well, and the livery owner was surprised when he only wanted twenty dollars for the horse. The man told him that he just needed to unload the animal and that twenty was plenty. That's when the livery man got suspicious."

"Was anything missing?" Tyler asked. "Was there any sign of what might have happened?"

Randy shook his head and took the cup of coffee his father handed him. "No, even the Christmas gifts Amy bought were safely stashed in the saddlebags. There was no sign of blood or anything else that might give us a clue."

"Well, then, she wasn't taken for the money," Tyler thought aloud.

"You think she was taken then?" Charles asked, pouring a cup of the steaming liquid for Tyler.

Tyler nodded. "More so now than ever. If she'd gone out ahead of Angie and gotten hurt or lost her way somehow, the horse would have come on home. Nobody is missing in town, but that still leaves the area surrounding it. Were any of the local men interested in Amy? I mean would they have taken her by force?"

"Naw." Charles shook his head and made a face, as though the thought was ridiculous. "We've been here a long time, Tyler. Ain't no one round here who would try to get a woman that way. Besides, I don't know anyone who was even interested in Amy. You know how it is between Angie and Amy. Angie's always courting and Amy never was. The only one marginally interested in her was Jacob Anderson and he's been most devoted to helping us look for her."

"If someone did take her," Randy began, "and I'm inclined to believe someone did, what reason could they possibly have had? What purpose would it serve to take Amy?"

"That's what I'm trying to figure out," Tyler replied softly. He took a long drink from the mug and set it on the table. "By my calculations there is only about an hour on the day Amy disappeared that her whereabouts was unaccounted for before Angie noticed her horse was gone. The time from which Amy left the store until Angie began looking for her was only forty-five minutes, maybe an hour at best. Somewhere in that hour is when Amy was taken. Since no one remembers seeing any strangers in town, Amy had to have been taken by someone familiar to her. Maybe she was even talked into helping someone she knew well and went willingly with them."

Charles rubbed his jaw, then looked at his son. Randy nodded; Tyler's words made sense.

"So what do we do from here?" Charles asked.

Tyler rubbed his own stubbly chin for a moment, noticing absently that he needed a shave. "We make a list," he finally said. "We make a list of everyone in the area. Then we plot the names on a map. You take part of it, Charles, Randy a part, and I'll take another part. I'll stick to the town, since I'm not all that familiar with the outlying farms. You and Randy can divide your lists with someone you trust, like the Andersons. Then we'll go door to door, farm to farm. We'll question everybody and leave no stone unturned."

Charles frowned. "That might make our neighbors feel we don't trust them to come forward with what they know."

"They'll understand." Tyler drained the coffee from his

cup, then added, "They won't be offended if you remind them that should this have happened to one of their own family members, you'd expect them to do the same."

"I'll get some paper," Charles agreed and left the room.

"I'll get the horses in the stable," Randy offered, "and then I'll help you map this thing out."

Tyler tried to ignore the anguish in his soul. He had forced his voice to remain calm and even while he talked with Randy and Charles, but inside he was gnawed by a fear that said if Amy's horse had turned up as far away as Hays, then Amy too could be long gone from Deer Ridge.

Running a hand through the waves of his hair, Tyler decided not to say anything to the family. No sense taking away what little hope they had. Tyler would keep the fear to himself that with each passing day, Amy was getting further and further from his reach. He whispered a prayer and sat down at the table, prepared to work.

❧

Making the list and map took them most of the evening. When it was completed, Tyler divided it in thirds, with the larger of the shares going to Charles and Randy.

"I'm heading home." Randy stuffed the paper in his pocket. "I'll be back early and we can get started then."

"We'll be ready," Charles replied and bid his son goodbye.

The silence that fell between Charles and Tyler was numbing. Each man wanted to comfort the other, but neither had any words for what they were feeling. Each bore a burden so heavy that the weight drained them of energy. Finally, Charles reached out and placed his hand over Tyler's. Tyler lifted his eyes and saw the tear-stained cheeks of a worried father.

"If God be for us," the pastor whispered, "who can be

against us?"

ò

Tyler spent a restless night in the Carmichaels' spare bedroom. He could hear Dora crying off and on from down
the hall, and from time to time Angie joined in from the
privacy of her own room. A verse from the Bible came to
Tyler, the verse that describes Rachel weeping for her
children and refusing to be comforted. The verse so
haunted Tyler that at last he got up and opened his Bible
to Jeremiah 31:15.

"Thus saith the Lord; A voice was heard in Ramah, lam-
entation, and bitter weeping; Rachel weeping for her children refused to be comforted, because they were not."

Tyler shuddered, but then he found the Lord leading his
eyes on to verses sixteen and seventeen, and the words he
read now brought him hope.

"Thus saith the Lord; Refrain thy voice from weeping,
and thine eyes from tears: for thy work shall be rewarded,
saith the Lord; and they shall come again from the land of
the enemy. And there is hope in thine end, saith the Lord,
that thy children shall come again to their own border."
He read the words silently, then again aloud.

A weight lifted from his shoulders, and he fell to his
knees in prayer. First he offered thanksgiving for the scrip-
tures God had led him to, and then he began to petition
his Father for Amy's safety.

ò

When Randy arrived the next morning, the entire family
gathered for Tyler to lead them in devotions and prayers.
He shared the precious verses he'd read the night before.
"We must put our hope in God," he reminded them. "He
is our only hope right now, but He won't let us down. He
is the only One Who can reach out and help Amy. We

must put her in His hands." Tyler waited for them to absorb his words, and then he added, "We can trust Him with Amy's life, for He loves her even more than we ever will."

At these words, Dora seemed to sit straighter and even Angie lost her mask of fear. A light had been given them in their darkness, and they stood at a crossroads that would lead them to a wonderous peace of mind.

"You're right, Tyler," Charles said finally. "We've been fighting this thing too hard on our own. If we're to ever get anywhere, we must let God work it out." Angie, Dora and Randy nodded in unison.

≈

After breakfast the men readied their horses and prepared to leave. Dora and Angie stood by helplessly watching, until Angie could no longer stand it.

"Can't I go along and help?" she asked her father.

"No, you'd best stay here. We still don't know what we're going to find out there. I'd rather you be here to care for your mother." Charles gave Angie's cheek a gentle stroke.

"But it's awful just waiting here," she protested.

Dora nodded. "Feels like we're not doing our part."

"Somebody should be here," Tyler said before Charles could reply. "In case Amy makes it home on her own. If you're both here, then Angie can ride out and let the rest of us know."

"I suppose that makes sense." Dora put her arm around Angie. "And," she added softly, "we can continue to pray."

Angie saw the wisdom in their words, and though she longed to be at some other task, she agreed that they needed to stay at the house.

"We'll be back by dark," Charles said, mounting his

horse. The cold leather creaked and groaned as he settled his body in the saddle. "Looks like it might snow again, so you'd best stay inside."

"What about the chores, Pa?" Angie questioned.

"We took care of everything before you ladies got up. You just stick indoors and stay warm," Charles instructed. He hated to leave them alone, but he knew he had to trust God to watch over them if he was to go look for his other daughter. He gave Dora a loving look and then turned his horse to follow Randy and Tyler across the yard.

"Kind of like leaving the ninety-nine," he murmured aloud.

"What was that?" Tyler questioned.

Charles smiled and pulled up even with Tyler. "I was just thinking that leaving them here is like the shepherd who leaves the ninety-nine to go look for the one."

Tyler returned the smile with a nod. "That it is. I guess now we know just how precious that one can be."

thirteen

Tyler stood in the center of Deer Ridge's Main Street and stared down at the list. He decided to start with Miller's Hotel, since six of the people on his list resided there. He spoke first to Mr. and Mrs. Miller and then was happily received by Marvin Williams, who was enjoying his holiday break from teaching.

Marvin, however, knew next to nothing about the entire affair, and so Tyler moved on to Nathan Gallagher's room. He knocked, but receiving no answer from the other side of the door, he again moved on. He could pin Gallagher down at his office later, he decided.

The town barber and dentist, Newt Bramblage, was also absent from the hotel, but Mrs. Miller reminded Tyler that he'd probably be happy to answer any questions while giving Tyler a shave.

The only other resident was an elderly woman who rarely left her room. The woman had a delicate constitution, and so as not to upset her unduly, Mrs. Miller questioned her for Tyler. The woman, not surprisingly, had no knowledge of Amy Carmichael's whereabouts; she went still further, however, and insisted that since she was not given to gossip, she would have nothing to share in the future, even in the unlikely event that she should fall privy to such knowledge.

Tyler thanked the Millers and moved on down the street to where Doc Taggert was shoveling snow in front of his building. "Doc," Tyler called and climbed down from his horse. He tied the reins and offered to take over the shoveling if Doc would speak to him about Amy. He finished the remaining work quickly, and Doc invited him inside for coffee and biscuits.

"My wife Gretta always worries that I'll starve before I come home for lunch." Doc smiled. "Then she wonders why I don't have much of an appetite at supper."

Tyler laughed and helped himself to the offered refreshment. "I'll happily share your misery." He bit into a fluffy biscuit.

"I don't know what I can do to help you." Doc took a seat behind his desk. "I don't believe I saw Amy at all the day she disappeared."

"Did you work in your office that day?"

"Sure did," Doc replied. "I was here pert near all day. I'd just gotten in a shipment of medicine and had to inventory it before I could close up and go home. I was just leaving when—say, wait a minute."

Tyler leaned forward. "What is it, Doc?"

"I didn't see Amy that day," Doc said thoughtfully, "but I did see Angie."

"Oh." Tyler sat back hard against the wooden chair. The disappointment was clear on his face.

"Yes," Doc remembered. "She was just crossing the street and heading into Nathan Gallagher's office when I was locking my front door."

Tyler leaned forward again. "You saw Angie going into Nathan's office?"

"That's right."

"How did you know it was Angie? I'd think from a distance it would be pretty hard to tell the twins apart. I'm not sure even I could do it. What made you so sure it was Angie and not Amy?"

Doc shrugged and scratched his jaw. "I guess I just assumed it was Angie. After all, Amy wouldn't have any reason to visit Gallagher. He's not at all her type. Besides, everybody knows Angie considers him one of her more serious gentlemen callers."

"But—" Tyler opened his mouth, then closed it again. His eyes narrowed, and he took a deep breath. "You're sure it was the same day that Amy disappeared?"

"Positive."

Tyler grabbed his hat. "Thanks, Doc. I think you've helped me a great deal."

Without another word, Tyler hurried from Doc's office. He left his horse behind and walked to Nathan's office. Nathan had insisted that he'd not seen Angie or Amy on the day Amy disappeared—and now Tyler had proof that he'd lied.

"Gallagher!" Tyler slammed the office door behind him.

Nathan came from the inner office with the same look of surprise that he'd worn the visit before. "What in the world is going on, Preacher?"

"Doc Taggert says he saw Angie come here to visit you the day Amy disappeared." Tyler's voice was flat.

Nathan's mouth hardened. "He's mistaken, Andrews. I told you that I didn't see Angie that day."

Tyler stepped forward, barely able to control his temper. "Doc was sure about what he'd seen."

"Doc is an old man." Nathan laughed. "He simply has his days mixed up. Angie never came to see me that day." Nathan's voice was confident. The more time that passed, the closer he was to accomplishing his goal of robbing the town on Christmas. Without a clue to Amy's whereabouts, Andrews was simply grasping at straws.

"I'm going to get to the bottom of this." Tyler's tone

left Nathan little doubt that he would do just that.

"Well, you aren't going to get to the bottom of it here," Nathan replied.

Tyler backed away, fearful that if he remained within punching distance of Nathan, he'd lose control and flatten the man. "I'll be back." He looked at Nathan for another moment, his eyes dark with anger.

"You do that, Preach." Nathan crossed his arms across his chest and smiled. "I'll be here—and I won't have any more information for you then than I do now."

Tyler stalked out of the office and climbed into his saddle with a growl that made his horse's eyes roll. Tyler knew that Gallagher was keeping something from him, but he had no proof. His only recourse was to head back to the farm and question Angie. Perhaps she'd lied about seeing Gallagher for fear her folks wouldn't like her forward actions. Maybe she *had* seen him and covering that up made her feel even guiltier about Amy. Tyler shook his head and urged his mount forward. He would have to question Angie in private and promise to keep her secret.

≈

Amy forced herself to wake up, but the effort cost her every ounce of determination she had. She was weak from lack of food and numb from the growing cold. She had no idea how much time had passed, and so she tried to concentrate on the present moment only. She could not anticipate the future, and remembering the past now only made the present seem worse. She was no longer living even one day at a time; instead, she knew if she was to survive she must live moment by moment.

She wasn't worrying anymore about whether Nathan would steal the harvest money. Now she thought only of whether or not he would free her before she succumbed to cold and thirst.

Each minute seemed as long as an hour. She still had a little water left, but she was afraid her thirst would drive her to swallow the remaining drops in one gulp. Again and again she reached out to take the jar in her hand, but each time she forced herself to put it back on the table. She had to make the water last. Without water, she would surely die.

With each passing moment, the room seemed smaller, as though the walls were closing in on her. She tried the door over and over, and shouted until her voice was hoarse. The longer she considered her plight, the more certain she felt that Nathan intended to leave her to die. Finally, her desperation drove her to action.

"My only hope of getting out of here is through the roof," she said aloud. She took the lamp and water from the table and put them on the floor. Next, she looked around the room, trying to figure out where the roof might be the weakest and easiest to penetrate. She moved the table to one side and gingerly tested it to see if it would hold her.

The table wobbled, but it held as Amy put her full weight on it. Weakly, she climbed to her feet on the tabletop and then had to duck down to keep from hitting the ceiling overhead. She pulled at the cold, packed dirt with her hands until she cried out from the pain. The dirt was frozen by the winter's cold, and Amy's numb fingers were no match for it.

Glancing around the room, Amy looked for some tool to make her job easier. She found nothing that looked promising, though, and so she continued to labor with her hands. God would give her strength, she reminded herself. "God is my strength," she whispered again and again while she scrabbled with her numb hands at the frozen ceiling. "God is my strength."

&

Tyler pushed his overworked gelding to gallop across the prairie until they reached the Carmichael farm. Tyler dismounted quickly and left his mount in the barn. He knew he should care for the horse, but the snow was coming down heavier than before and time was of the essence. He patted the patient animal apologetically and turned toward the house.

Before he could reach the door, Angie burst through it. "What is it? Did you find her?" she cried. "Mother is sleeping, but I can wake her."

"No, Angie." Tyler pulled her into the house with him. "I have to talk to you alone. It's very important."

Angie's brow wrinkled. "Me? Why me?"

"Sit here with me." Tyler pulled one of the kitchen chairs out for Angie.

Angie did as he asked, but her apprehension mounted with each silent moment that passed. Finally, Tyler found the right words to begin.

"Angie, I know this might be a delicate matter to broach, but if it weren't so important, I assure you I would never question what you told me before." Tyler took a deep breath. "Doc Taggert and I talked this morning. It seems he remembers you going to Nathan's office the afternoon Amy disappeared."

Angie shook her head. "I already told you that I didn't see Nathan that day. I spent my time with Mrs. Miller. I let Amy think I was going to go calling on some of my beaus—but that was just so she wouldn't suspect the Christmas present for her I was planning with Mrs. Miller. Mrs. Miller can tell you I was with her the whole afternoon."

"Yes, she did say that." Tyler sighed. "Look Angie, I'm not calling you a liar—I'm just desperate to know the truth. If you went to Nathan's and felt ashamed—or if you were concerned about your folks—or one of your other beaus—catching wind of it, I promise to keep it to myself. It's just that when I questioned Gallagher about it, he swore to me that he'd not seen you either. And yet he acts suspicious about the whole thing. I need proof that he's lying to me."

"You think he's hiding something?" Angie asked in surprise.

"Could be. Is he hiding your visit?" Tyler's tone was gentle. "Is he protecting you, Angie?"

Angie shook her head vigorously. "No! I did not go to see Nathan Gallagher that day. I would have if I'd had time after I finished with Mrs. Miller, but I lost track of the time. By the time I returned to the store, Amy was already gone. I figured she'd be back soon, and so I finished my shopping. When she still hadn't come back, I decided to find her. I stepped outside the store and saw that her horse was still there, so I knew she was near by. That's when I went to talk to Ed. . ."

"Wait a minute, Angie," Tyler interrupted. "You just said that when you came out of the store, Amy's horse was still there."

Angie looked at him in astonishment. "Yes! Yes, it was there! That's why I went to ask Ed if he'd seen her. He was outside locking up and—oh, Tyler, what does it mean?"

Tyler got to his feet. "I don't know yet. What I do know is that Doc is confident that he saw you entering Nathan's office."

"But I didn't," Amy insisted.

"If you didn't," Tyler took a deep breath, "then it had to have been Amy that Doc saw!"

"Of course." Angie's eyes narrowed thoughtfully. "And if Amy went to Nathan's to find me, and Nathan swears he didn't see either of us, then he's lying. And that means he probably has done something with Amy."

"That's just about the way I figure it," Tyler muttered. "Tell me, Angie, has Nathan said anything to you about leaving town?"

Angie started to shake her head and then stopped abruptly. "He did say he wouldn't be here at Christmas. I remember, because I asked him to accompany me to your service and the festivities afterwards and he told me he couldn't."

"Did he say where he was headed?" Tyler moved closer to Angie and put his hands on her shoulders. "Think hard, Angie. Did he give you any idea at all?"

Angie thought for moment and then shook her head. "No. He just told me he couldn't escort me and left it at that. I wish I could be more help." She sniffed back tears. "That lying, no good skunk. He better not have hurt my sister. I just wish there was something I could do to help her."

Tyler put his arm around her and patted her shoulder. "It's all right, Angie. You've given me more to go on than anyone else. You've at least pointed the way. Now listen to me carefully. I want you to wake your mother and tell her what we know. Then I want you to ride out and find your father. It's snowing again, so dress warm and ride quickly."

"What do you want me to tell him?"

"Tell him to find Randy and meet me in town. Since Nathan's still in town and Christmas is tomorrow, he must be planning to make his break tonight. We'll have to be there to follow him and hope that he'll lead us to Amy."

Angie dried her tears and agreed to Tyler's plan. "I'll send them, don't worry about a thing. Just please, please find Amy."

"I'll do my best," Tyler promised, heading for the door. "You just do what I've told you and keep praying."

fourteen

Tyler went straight to Nathan's office, but he found it dark and the door locked. He glanced down the darkening street to the boarding house, wondering if Nathan had taken refuge in his room, or if he had fled town altogether. Tyler could only pray that he'd not find the latter to be the case.

"Pastor Andrews," a voice called from behind him, and Tyler turned to find Jeremy Smith.

"Evening." Tyler's manner was preoccupied.

"Gallagher's gone home for the night," Jeremy said, gesturing toward the locked office. "I saw him leave not ten minutes ago for the boarding house."

Tyler let out all his breath at once. "I guess I'll talk to him later," he said and started for his horse.

"Pastor," Jeremy called out, "you will be giving us a service tomorrow, won't you?"

Tyler turned and saw that several other people had joined Jeremy. "Yeah, Pastor," another man added, "the family's sure been looking forward to Christmas morning service."

Tyler had nearly forgotten his promise to preach. His worry for Amy was shutting out all other thought. "I'll be there," he replied, knowing that his voice lacked its normal enthusiasm.

"Good, good," Jeremy said, satisfied that the matter was settled. "The kids are going to put on a play for us, and I've got sacks of candy to give them after you preach. It's going to be a lot of fun for them. I know you're mighty worried about Amy, but I wouldn't want to spoil things for the young 'uns."

Tyler agreed that they should not spoil the festivities, but his heart wasn't in his words. He knew only God could mend the hurt that bound him inside.

Excusing himself, he pushed past the men and got on his horse. "I'll see you all tomorrow morning." He rode out past the hotel, casting a suspicious glance upward at the second story windows.

He manuevered his horse into the shadows of nearby trees and dismounted. From where he stood, he could watch the boarding house, and he realized that he might learn more by waiting for Nathan to move than by questioning him further.

Grateful that the snow had let up, Tyler decided to board his horse at the livery and stake out the boarding house from the livery loft. From there, he would have a view of everything around, and he'd be able to spot Randy and Charles when they made their way to join him.

❧

If the livery owner thought the new pastor was strange for wanting to sleep in the loft, he made no mention of it as he accepted Tyler's money.

Tyler saw to his horse's care and feed, then threw his saddle bags over his shoulder and made his way up the rough ladder to the loft. Tossing the bags aside, Tyler eased the heavy wooden shutter open just enough to peer down the road. All seemed quiet. Only the soft glow from the windows of the surrounding homes broke the fall of darkness.

Tyler studied the boarding house a moment longer, noting the side stairs that led to the second floor. Gallagher would have to come out one of three ways, Tyler surmised. Either by the front or back door or these side stairs.

Whichever he chose, Tyler was ready.

Tyler was prepared for a lengthy stay, but within a half an hour, he was rewarded by the appearance of Nathan Gallagher on the side stairs. He watched as Nathan moved away from the hotel and came toward the livery. Tyler wondered if Nathan had chosen to depart Deer Ridge now. Easing away from the window, Tyler heard the livery door open below. He held his breath.

After a moment, crawling at a snail's pace on his hands and knees, he eased his six foot six frame to the edge of the loft. Looking over, Tyler flattened himself in the straw and watched the dark hatted head below. Nathan seemed to be waiting for someone to appear. He checked his watch several times and paced the floor below, making the horses stir.

Tyler could hardly force himself to remain still. He kept thinking of Amy and wondered if Nathan had hurt her. Every time her brown eyes and smiling mouth came to mind, Tyler had to bite back a growl. He wanted to throttle the man, but he knew Gallagher's type wouldn't respond to force. Lord, I need patience and steadfastness, Tyler prayed. Feeling the cold bite into his skin, he could only hope that Nathan would lead him to Amy soon.

The back door to the livery swung open then, and a man appeared in the shadowy light. Tyler saw that he matched the description of the man who had sold Amy's horse.

"Gallagher?" the man called, and Nathan stepped into the light.

"Here," he replied. "Did you do the job?"

"You paid me to do it, didn't you?" the man growled. "Still can't figure selling a fine piece of horseflesh like that for only twenty dollars. Why, the saddle alone. . ."

"I don't want to hear what you think," Nathan interrupted. "That's precisely why your brother isn't working with us any more. Because he thought too much."

"Well, what do you want me to do now?" the man asked.

"Come back to my room with me. We'll take the side stairs and no one will see you." Nathan motioned the man to leave the way he'd come.

Tyler wished he could follow them, but he knew he wouldn't have enough cover to get close enough where he could be out of sight and still hear the conversation. All he could do was watch the two men walk away, knowing full well that one or both of them knew where his beloved Amy was hidden.

The men had no sooner disappeared into the hotel then Tyler spotted two riders approaching. He figured they would be Randy and Charles, and he bounded down the ladder to meet them in the street before they could go in search of him.

The Carmichael men were anxious for whatever news Tyler could share. He told them what little he knew, including the whereabouts of the man who'd sold Amy's horse. He and Charles had to grab Randy's shoulders to keep him from storming over and calling the man into the street.

"It won't get Amy back," Tyler insisted, while Charles kept a firm grip on his son's arm.

"Tyler's right," Charles said. "You can't just barge in over there and spill your guts. If Tyler is right, and Nathan plans to make some move between now and the morning, we'll be here to see what it is."

"Each of us needs to stake out a different spot," Tyler suggested. "I'll bet Doc would let one of you use his place."

"We'll work that out, Tyler," Charles agreed. "You stay here and we'll do what we have to."

"If anyone sees or hears anything that bears notifying the others about, don't waste any time. We may only have minutes to act." Tyler's voice was grave.

Randy nodded and swallowed his anger. "I hope your plan works."

Tyler looked first at Randy and then Charles. "I pray it does, too."

~

Loneliness settled over Tyler after Charles and Randy had gone. Whenever he was near Amy's family, he felt at least a small link with her, but now nothing distracted him from the image of Amy cold and afraid somewhere, perhaps hurt, needing him. . . Nothing could comfort him.

No, that wasn't true, he realized as he settled himself in the loft again. God was with him and God was with Amy. That was comfort enough.

An hour passed before the scraggly looking man reappeared on the side stairs of the boarding house. Tyler watched the darkness, straining to see where the man would go next. He was surprised to see him return to the livery.

Without thought for his safety, Tyler perched himself on the edge of the loft landing and waited for the man to appear. The door groaned as it was pushed open and then closed with a thud. The man had taken only two or three steps when Tyler jumped from the loft and threw his full weight against him. Delivering a well placed blow to the burly man's face, Tyler knocked him nearly senseless.

Tyler quickly bound the stranger's hands and feet, hoping he could finish before the man's head cleared. His task accomplished, Tyler manuevered the heavy man to one side of the livery and went for a bucket of water to revive him.

The frigid water made the man jump, and his eyes flew open. "What the—" The man noticed Tyler for the first time. "Who are you, mister?"

"I'm Tyler Andrews, the circuit rider for these parts. I'm also the man who hopes to marry Amy Carmichael as soon as she's found," Tyler replied.

The man shook his head. "Don't know no Amy Carmichael." He reached his tied hands up to his bruised jaw. "Why'd you do this? Sure don't seem like a very parson-like thing for you to be doing."

Tyler studied the man carefully. He seemed to be genuinely surprised that Tyler would have any interest in him. "I know you're working with Nathan Gallagher. And I know you sold Amy's horse in Hays."

"I did sell a horse for Gallagher," the man admitted, "but I didn't know who it belonged to. He just told me to get rid of it quick-like and I did."

"It doesn't matter." Tyler drew closer. "What does matter is that you'd best tell me where Gallagher has Amy and you'd best tell me right now."

The man shook his head. "I'm telling you, mister, I don't know any Amy. There ain't been any woman involved in my dealings with Gallagher."

Tyler grabbed the man by the collar and yanked him forward. "Then you'd best tell me what you and Gallagher are up to and let me judge for myself."

The man's eyes narrowed, as if he were considering Tyler's words. "I don't reckon Mister Gallagher would like that," he finally replied.

Tyler's face twisted. He tightened his grip on the man and slammed him back against the wall. "I don't reckon

Gallagher's going to take the beating that you are when I go across the street and retrieve Amy's pa and brother. Of course, that's going to be after I get done with you myself. After that, I figure you'll be right glad to go to the gallows."

The man blanched. He wasn't getting paid enough by Gallagher to take the gallows for him. Especially if Gallagher had done in some woman in the process of setting up his scheme. Looking into the preacher's face, the man met his deadly stare. What he saw there was more than enough to unnerve him.

"I'll talk," the red-headed man declared. "I ain't going to hang for something I ain't done."

"You'd best get to it then." Tyler voice was ominously calm.

"Gallagher plans to rob the bank tomorrow morning," the man replied. "He has the combination to the safe and while the town is celebrating Christmas at the school, he's going to let himself in and clean out the harvest money."

Tyler nodded. The man's explanation made everything fall into place. Somehow, Amy must have overheard Gallagher's plans. That was why he had taken her hostage. At last her disappearance was starting to make some sense.

"How do you and your brother figure in this?" Tyler asked, surprising the man with his reference to his brother.

Rather than question the preacher, though, since the huge man seemed to be feeling a might testy, the red-haired man hurried to answer his question. "We arranged to get Gallagher's stuff out of town. Then we were to act as lookouts while Gallagher took the money. We aren't involved in any killings, though, and I never did see any woman. That's the God's honest truth, preacher."

"Gallagher never said anything about a woman over-hearing his plans? He never told you that the horse belonged to Amy Carmichael?"

"No, sir, he never told me nothing. He got mad at my brother and told him to git. Told me I could have his cut if I wanted to keep on with the plan. It sounded like easy money, so I told him I would. When he told me to take the horse to Hays, he just told me to get rid of it without a scene and to take whatever I could get without haggling the price. I did that and came back here to let him know and get ready for tomorrow."

Tyler realized the man was most likely telling the truth. He studied him for a moment before speaking. "So you aren't supposed to see Gallagher again until tomorrow?"

"I ain't supposed to meet up with him until after the job's done," the man admitted. "I'm supposed to wait between the bank and the school and make sure no one interrupts Gallagher. After that, I'm supposed to ride out and meet him at the river."

Tyler nodded. "Good enough. I'm going to have to lock you up, but maybe once this is done with—and if Miss Carmichael is found, unharmed—just maybe the judge will go easy on you for cooperating with me."

The man grumbled at Tyler's plan, but he knew he had nothing to bargain. He nodded weakly and resigned himself to captivity.

Tyler locked the man in the tack room and hurried to find Charles and Randy. He located Charles first and together they went to retrieve Randy. He quickly explained to them what he knew.

"Look," Tyler said, the excitement clear in his voice. "Gallagher plans to rob the bank tomorrow while we're having Christmas service. We've got to play this thing out carefully and give him no reason to believe that anything is amiss. Most likely he'll be ready to use Amy as insurance for his plans."

"What'll we do?" Charles asked cautiously.

"We'll act as though nothing has changed," Tyler said. "Randy, you go on home to your family and, Charles, you do the same. Get everybody up and around for the services and bring them on in, just like you planned."

"We can't just pretend nothing's happened," Randy protested.

"Of course we can." Tyler's firmness hushed Randy's objection. "It's the only way we can smoke Gallagher out of his hole."

"The Andersons will need to know," Charles said. "They've been so good to help look for Amy. I know they'd want to be in on this."

"Good. In fact," Tyler had a sudden thought, "we'll need Ed to be inside the bank before Gallagher gets there."

"What do you have in mind?" Charles asked. He looked at the preacher and shook his head, and his lips curled a little. "Never would have thought no parson could be as mean as you are."

"Even Christ got angry enough to physically throw the money changers out of the Temple," Tyler answered. "When He saw true evil, He was just as 'mean' as I feel today."

"What do you have in mind?" Charles repeated.

Tyler smiled, feeling assurance for the first time. He'd finally nailed Gallagher down. "Well, I see it like this. . ."

fifteen

The sleepy people of Deer Ridge emerged from the warmth of their homes and made their way to the school house for Christmas morning services. Tyler stood outside the school welcoming the families as though nothing was amiss. He saw pain and fear in the eyes of some of the people and wished he could ease their minds even a portion.

Wagons came rattling in from the farthest reaches, and those who dared to make the snowy trip were anxious to seek the warmth of the school building. Dora and Angie Carmichael arrived well bundled in the buckboard, with Charles riding along side. Close behind them was Randy and his family in their wagon, with Randy's horse tied on the back. Tyler nodded to the two Carmichael men and felt a calm assurance that everything was falling into place.

He cast a quick glance down the street to where the bank stood. Ed Anderson had taken up his place there some hours earlier, and Tyler knew that the other Anderson men were waiting out of sight in order to lend a hand in the capture of Nathan Gallagher. All was progressing as planned.

"Let's hurry inside, folks," Tyler called to the gathering crowd. "We've got a good fire going in the stove and Brother Smith has kindly furnished hot cider for everyone."

The children clapped their hands at this, and the adults offered brief smiles of gratitude. Tyler knew their discouragement and worry. Wasn't his own heart nearly broken? Didn't his own mind strike against him with torturous thoughts that Amy might already be dead?

Please, Father, he prayed silently, help me be strong for these people. Help me to help them through this. And be with Amy wherever she is. Let her know that help is on its way—that we haven't forgotten her.

⋟

Amy struggled to climb again onto the table. She had little strength left to even walk, much less to put forth the energy required to knock a hole in the roof. She had no way of knowing how much time had passed, but in spite of the care she had taken, she was out of water now, and the lamp was nearly out of oil.

Always before, Amy had forced herself to ignore her dilemma and to concentrate instead on the task at hand. Minute by minute, she reminded herself that she could lie down and die, or fight to escape. Up until this moment, she had always chosen quickly to fight. Now, however, she was tired, cold, hungry, and completely defeated in spirit.

"God," she whispered in a hoarse voice, "I know You're here." She felt like crying, but tears had long since stopped coming. "I've got nothing else to give, Lord. I'm spent and we both know it."

Just then a huge clod of dirt worked loose from the roof and fell, striking Amy across the face. The pain it caused was brief, but the sunlight it let in was stunning.

Amy stared up in disbelief at the small hole. Bits of snow came in with the dirt, and Amy instantly reached out to pull a handful of the moist whiteness into her mouth. Her lips and tongue seemed to suck up the snow instantly, and eager for more, Amy reached out again and again.

The stream of sunlight offered only shadowy light to

the room, but it was enough to encourage Amy. She felt as though God had spoken to her directly, and she worked at the hole with fresh strength, scraping and clawing, until all of her fingers were cut and bleeding.

But she was too weak to work for very long. When her legs would hold her no longer, Amy let herself sink down on the tabletop to rest. After a moment, she rolled from its surface and took herself to the bed, hoping to regain even a little more strength so that she could continue her work.

She closed her eyes and felt the air grow colder. She hadn't thought about the fact that by making a hole in the roof, she would lose what little warmth she'd maintained in the dugout. Opening her eyes, Amy glanced up at her handiwork, then sat up abruptly. Her newfound hope ebbed into despair. The hole was hardly more than eight inches across, too small to do her any practical good. All of her hard work had rendered nothing more than this!

She began to sob, though her eyes refused to produce tears, and she slumped down again on the bed. Hopeless despair filled her heart and all reasonable thought left her mind.

"I'm going to die," she cried. "Oh, God, I can't bear this!"

Her body was spent, and she had no energy left to urge her on. For a moment longer she struggle to call forth the will to fight, but then at last she gave up and offered God her life, praying that death would be quick and painless.

The exhaustion of the past week had overtaken her, and she had no strength left to fight death any longer. Without even bothering to pull the filthy cover around her, Amy let her mind drift into dreams of her family and Tyler.

It must close to Christmas, she thought. Will they still

have the Christmas service? Will they sing the old songs? she wondered.

Strains of music rose through her memories. The haunting melody of Silent Night brought her tired mind peace. "All is calm, all is bright." She mouthed the words. "Sleep in Heavenly peace." Yes, she thought. I will sleep in Heavenly peace.

꒜

Tyler stood at the front of the school room for only a moment. He looked out at the community gathered there, and then he made a brief statement. When he had finished, stunned silence echoed through the room.

"You must help us," Tyler beseeched the crowd. "Amy Carmichael's life depends on it. I don't mind telling you good folks, her life has come to mean a great deal to me."

Several couples exchanged brief knowing smiles before they turned back to the preacher, awaiting further instruction. Moments later the congregation joined in song. The music rang out loudly as Mrs. Smith played a donated piano, and the gathering did their part to assure anyone listening from outside that the service was well underway.

Meanwhile, Tyler hurried out the back door and came quietly around the school to where his horse was hitched. In one fluid movement, he pulled the reins loose and mounted the animal's back. Then, without making a sound, he pushed the horse into a gallop across the snow-covered plain.

꒜

Nathan heard the singing and knew his time had come. He smiled and congratulated himself on the simplicity of his plan. He was Morgan Stewart's lawyer, and Morgan Stewart was the bank's owner. He was also the only one besides Ed Anderson who had the combination to the safe. That was he *was* the only one before he had hired Nathan as his lawyer. Then he had allowed Nathan to keep the carefully guarded secret in a confidential file with Stewart's other important papers.

The whole thing had been too simple, Nathan laughed. He'd only had to place himself in the community for a couple of years and earn their regard and trust. Then when the opportunity of a good harvest presented itself, Nathan knew his time had come.

He threw the last of his belongings into already bulging saddlebags and made his way down the side stairs of the hotel. He would miss Mrs. Miller's apple dumplings, he thought, but with thousands of dollars in his keep, he could no doubt buy tasty apple dumplings elsewhere.

He went to the livery and saddled his horse, loading his bags before leading the animal down the empty street. The bank sat there like an unguarded jewel, and Nathan felt his pulse quicken.

Down the street, the townspeople broke into yet another Christmas carol, oblivious to the evil that lurked just steps away. At least that's what Nathan presumed.

Quickly, he hitched the horse behind the bank. He looked up and down the empty alleyway, and then with great caution, he picked the lock on the bank door and let himself in.

With the door closed behind him, the singing voices were muted. He steadied his nerves with a deep breath and moved toward the safe. One step, then two, and everything was quiet, just as it should be. But as he lifted his foot a third time, a voice stopped him cold.

"Hello, Gallagher." Ed Anderson sat ever so casually to one side of the room, contemplating the revolver he held in his hand.

Nathan's eyes narrowed and he whirled on his heel, his own gun quickly drawn from his coat pocket. "Anderson!" He leveled the pistol.

Ed seemed unmoved. His sober gaze never wavered. "Where's Amy?"

Nathan had forgotten the girl, and now he nearly laughed. "Somewhere you'll never find her."

"Now, that doesn't seem to be a very reasonable way to act," Ed said.

Nathan sneered. "Drop your gun, Anderson. I have a quicker hand than you, and I won't hesitate to shoot."

"Oh?" Ed raised a brow. "Then you won't mind when the whole town is alerted by the noise?"

Nathan realized Ed was right. He paused a moment to rethink his plan. "Where's the money?" he asked, noticing that the safe was open.

"Where's Amy?"

But Gallagher refused to give in, and Ed realized he'd have to draw him out. "Look," Ed began, "we know you're using Amy as your protection. I realize that once you leave here, you'll go get her and force her to ride with you so that none of us will follow."

Nathan smiled smugly. Anderson had just given him his new plan of action. "That's right. If you try to stop me, Amy will die."

"I kind of figured that." Ed's voice was cool. "I just figured maybe you'd strike a deal. Like I give you the money and you give me Amy. Maybe we could have a trade off down by the river."

"No," Nathan refused firmly. "I'm not a fool to fall into a predictable plan like that. You'll give me the money now and you won't follow me—or you'll never see Amy

Carmichael again!"

Ed got to his feet and took a step toward Gallagher. The look on his face was threatening, and Nathan waved him back with the gun. "If I have to, I'll shoot you—whether the town hears me or not. When they come running, I'll just tell them that I stopped you from robbing the bank. Of course, you'll be dead and dead men tell no tales. Then where will your precious Amy be?"

"All right, Gallagher," Ed said between his clenched teeth, "you win."

"Of course I do. Now, give me the money and leave me to ride out of here. Remember, I'll have the girl and there won't be anything to stop me from killing her."

Ed nodded and motioned to the safe. "The money's still inside."

"Get it," Nathan commanded and stepped back. "But first, lose that gun."

Ed looked angrily at Gallagher for a moment and then put the gun down on the desk top. He crossed the room to the safe and pulled out two full money bags.

"Put them on the table by the door," Nathan motioned, and Ed did as he was told. "Now, get down on your belly and don't even think of following me. Not if you want me to release the Carmichael girl unharmed."

Ed began to get down on the floor. "What assurance do I have that she hasn't already been harmed?" he asked.

"None." Nathan leered. "But what other choice do you have?"

Ed shrugged his shoulders and lay down on the floor. He waited until Nathan had grabbed up the money and exited the bank before raising his head. Then glancing around cautiously to make certain Gallagher wasn't waiting for him, Ed got to his feet, pulled on his coat, and ran out of the bank.

He mounted his horse and circled the building. Gallagher was long gone, much to Ed's relief, but the tracks in the snow pointed the direction he'd fled, and Ed knew that his brothers and Amy's family would already be tracking the man. Hopefully, he'd lead them straight to Amy.

sixteen

Amy's mind registered sounds, but she told herself she was dreaming. She thought she heard a horse's whinny and the sound of movement on the ground above her, but try as she might, she couldn't push herself to investigate.

She forced her eyes open, only to be blinded by a flood of brilliant light as the door creaked open. She waited, uncertain whether she was dead or alive. Either way, she could only wait, helpless, for whatever happened next.

She felt herself being lifted, and for a moment she wondered if God had come to take her to Heaven. The thought comforted her, and she waited limp in the arms that bore her, hopeful that she'd find her celestial home on the other side of the door.

Instead, cold air hit her face, and Amy roused ever so slightly. Trying to focus on the face overhead, she felt a deep foreboding. This was definitely not her Heavenly Father who carried her.

"You didn't expect me to come back, did you?"

Amy shook her head, not in reply to the question, but because she was unsure of the words. Her mind was so muddled, clear thinking so beyond her strength, that she could only bide her time.

"The whole town has been looking for you," the voice said. "Especially that fool Andrews."

Amy's foggy mind grasped at the thought of Tyler Andrews. His name was like a lightning bolt, jolting her with energy. She remained silent, however, feigning the near unconscious state that she'd been in before. She still didn't have enough energy to fight this man, but no longer was she apathetic, ready to give up.

"Now," the voice spoke again, "everyone in town is going to have a little more to say about Nathan Gallagher."

Nathan! Of course, now Amy remembered. Nathan had brought her to the dugout. She forced her mind to remember the events, and through the clouds she pulled together bits and pieces. Yes, yes, she thought, I remember; Nathan planned to rob the bank.

All of a sudden Amy found herself slammed stomach side down against the back of a horse. Just as quickly, Nathan mounted behind her and half pulled her body across his lap.

"They won't be so inclined to do me in," he said with a laugh, "when they see what's at stake."

"I wouldn't count on that, Gallagher," a voice called.

Nathan whirled his mount around to meet the angry faces of Tyler Andrews and Randy and Charles Carmichael.

Tyler could barely maintain his seat at the sight of Amy, half-dead, sprawled across Nathan's lap. He gripped the reins so tight that both hands were balled into gloved fists. More than anything, he would have liked to strike those fists against Gallagher's head.

Randy Carmichael was feeling none too patient either. He moved his horse forward a step. "Let her go, Gallagher."

Nathan laughed and revealed his pistol. "I can easily shoot her," he replied, cocking the hammer. "And I will if you try to stop me from riding away from here."

"But then," Tyler's voice was steady, "you'd have no hostage. And instead of bank robbery, you'd be facing murder."

Nathan shrugged. "I don't intend to rot in any prison, either way."

The sound of Tyler's voice had cleared Amy's head a bit more. She moved it ever so slightly to get an idea of her circumstances. The tiny movement caught Tyler's eyes, but Nathan seemed not to notice.

I've got to keep him talking, thought Tyler. "Look Nathan," he began, surprising Charles and Randy with the smooth, open way he spoke, "this doesn't have to end badly. You know what you've done is wrong, but a lot of people have gone astray besides you. You know that God offers forgiveness and new life to all those who ask, no matter what they've done. Why not start over?"

"I don't need a sermon, Preach," Gallagher said.

Tyler moved his horse closer, his eyes never leaving Nathan's. "It's more than a sermon, Nathan, and you know it. If you died right now, you'd have to face God. Are you ready to do that? Are you ready to risk eternal damnation and separation from God?"

"I don't intend to die right now," Nathan said evenly.

"But you will if you don't hand Amy over," Randy promised, his voice tight.

Nathan shrugged. "But then you'd be responsible for her death."

Amy stiffened at the words being bandied over her head. Tyler's horse came forward another pace, making Nathan's horse prance nervously.

"Stay where you are, Andrews," Nathan demanded. "I know what you're trying—and it's not going to work."

"I'm not above begging." Tyler's voice was off-hand. "I don't want you to hurt her. I care a great deal about her. In fact, I love her and want her to be my wife."

Nathan laughed. "How touching. But I could care less."

"I guess I've pretty well figured that out." Tyler tried to control his temper. "Point is, I can't help trying. A man such as yourself must surely be in a position to understand that. After all, you're also facing a most precarious situation."

"I've had enough of this," Randy interrupted. He narrowed his eyes. "Gallagher, you let my sister go now or you'll have to deal with all of us."

"I thought I already was dealing with you," Nathan said, unmoved by Randy's declaration. "I seem to be managing satisfactorily." He grinned.

"Not quite." Ed Anderson came out of the trees. His brothers, Jacob and Jack, followed. Now six horsemen surrounded Nathan. Slowly he began to realize that he was losing the battle.

"God can still save your soul, Gallagher," Tyler edged the huge Morgan he rode another step forward. "But right now, you're the only one who can save your hide."

Nathan's horse shied at the Morgan's nearness and whinnied nervously. Tyler refused to back off and pressed his luck. Nathan quickly brought the gun up from Amy to level it at Tyler, just as the Morgan nudged his head against Gallagher's mount.

Amy took that opportunity to dig what was left of her ragged fingernails into the horse's side. Nathan's mount reared. While Nathan fought to hold onto the reins, Amy slid backward off the horse. She used every ounce of her remaining energy to roll to the side. After that, she could do nothing more than lie there and await her fate.

Without warning, Tyler leapt across his horse, knocking Nathan to the ground. The pistol fired harmlessly into the air as it flew from Nathan's hand. Within moments, four other men were helping to restrain Gallagher, while Charles Carmichael jumped to the ground and lifted Amy into his arms.

"Pa?" she whispered. Her throat was raw, and her voice was barely audible.

"I'm here, Amy," he answered with tears in his eyes. "You're safe now."

Tyler was at her side immediately. He pulled off his coat and wrapped it around her shivering body. In Amy's confused state of mind, she found his worried expression almost amusing, but the overgrown stubble of his beard amused her even more.

"You need a shave." She croaked the words against his ear.

Tyler lifted his head and laughed loud and hard, though tears shone in his eyes. Even Charles had to join in the laughter. "That's my girl," Tyler said, lifting her in his arms.

Randy left Nathan to the capable hands of the Andersons. They'd already agreed to be responsible for getting Gallagher to Hays. Ed was the one witness who would be able to confirm the bank robbery, and the others would no doubt be called upon if needed at a later date.

"Merry Christmas, Sis," Randy said, laying a hand on Amy's dirty cheek. Tears gleamed in Randy's eyes too.

"Quite a present," she replied weakly.

"Let's get her to Doc," Tyler said, heading for his horse with his precious cargo.

"I can take her," Randy offered. He reached out his arms, but his father's hand pulled him back.

"I think you'd have a fight on your hands if you tried to separate them now," Charles said softly.

Randy nodded. "I suppose you're right. If it were

Betsey. . ."

"Or Dora," Charles interjected. "There comes a time when fathers and brothers have to step aside. Now, come on, let's get back to town."

≈

Tyler held Amy close, whispering endearments and encouragement all the way back to Deer Ridge. She snuggled against the warmth of his coat, thanking God silently for sending help in time to rescue her from Nathan's plans.

She opened her eyes briefly and gazed up into the haggard face of the man she'd come to love more dearly than life. With a smile, she whispered, "I love you, Tyler Andrews."

Tyler shook his head with a grin. "You're something else, Amy Carmichael. You endure all of this and now you want to finally get around to telling me that you love me?"

"Just thought you'd like to hear it," she smiled, closing her eyes.

Tyler leaned down and placed a kiss against her forehead. "You bet I want to hear it. I want to hear it every day of my life for the rest of my life!"

≈

The entire town was waiting and watching for the riders to return. When they caught sight of Tyler's huge horse, they strained their eyes to identify the bundle he held. Cheers went up when Randy and Charles moved ahead to announce that Amy was alive, but extremely weak. Charles handed his reins to Randy and went quickly to Dora and Angie to assure them that Amy was safe. There were tears of joy on their faces as they followed arm in arm to Doc Taggert's office. In hushed conversation, the town's people gathered behind them and followed in the street to gather outside the doctor's office.

Tyler waited outside with Charles, while Dora and Angie went inside to be with Amy while Doc Taggert examined her.

"Where's Gallagher?" Jeremy Smith asked the question everyone wanted to know.

"The Andersons are taking him to Hays," Tyler replied. His mind was not on the question, though. He had been reluctant to leave Amy's side, and now he ached to know if she would be alright.

"Then he's alive?" someone else called out.

Randy moved through the crowd with Betsey at his side. Their children were being tended back at the school by one of the town's women, while baby Joey was safely tucked in the crook of his mother's arm.

"He's alive," Randy said, coming to stand beside his father. "He could just as well be dead and so could Amy, if it weren't for Tyler's patience." A smile crossed Randy's face. "Good thing for Gallagher, 'cause patience ain't exactly one of my own virtues."

The crowd laughed, and then Charles hushed them all. "I want to thank all of you for your help in finding Amy. We're stuck out here so far from everybody else in the world that we've truly become one big family. Without working together, we'd probably all perish."

Murmurs of agreement went through the crowd before Charles could speak again. "Truth is, and you folks need to understand this, Tyler Andrews saved this town from disaster. See Gallagher didn't just take Amy, he planned to clean out the bank as well. Amy overheard his plans and that's why he kidnapped her."

The exchange of looks between the people varied from

anger to plain shock. Their hopes and dreams were pinned on their savings and earnings.

"Look, I know you folks feel the same way I do about having a full-time parson around these parts. I think we pretty much owe that to Tyler and I'd like to propose we hire him on as Deer Ridge's first pastor." Charles sent a beaming smile toward the man he knew would one day be his son-in-law.

Cheers from the crowd confirmed that Deer Ridge's residents felt the same way the Carmichaels did.

"It's the least we can do," Jeremy Smith said to the crowd. "We wouldn't even have the money to last through the winter if it weren't for Andrews getting wind of Gallagher's plan."

"That's right," Mrs. Smith agreed enthusiastically. "I think Pastor Andrews is just what this town needs."

Tyler held out his hands to quiet the enthusiastic response of the people before him. "I appreciate the offer," he said.

"Well, what do you say?" Amos Osborne, Deer Ridge's self-appointed mayor, questioned Tyler. "Will you pastor our community? I'm sure I speak for all the folks here in saying we'd be most honored to have you stay on. We might even be able to build a church in another year or so—that is if we get another good year behind us." Everyone nodded in unison and waited for the towering man to speak.

Tyler's heart was touched, but his mind was on Amy. "I'll pray about it," he replied.

Just then Angie appeared at the door with a smile on her face. "Doc says Amy is half-starved and dehydrated. But she didn't suffer much from the cold, and he says she ought to be just fine in a few days."

Tyler reached out and gave Angie a hearty hug at the news.

"Whoa, preacher," someone called. "You got the wrong sister!" Everyone laughed, and Tyler's face reddened.

"Don't worry," Angie laughed. "I'll pass that hug on to the right one." With a wink, she turned and went back into the building.

๛

Bit by bit, the crowd dispersed and regathered at the schoolhouse where the festivities for Christmas started anew. Once Tyler was certain Amy was out of any real danger, he agreed to return and preach the service he'd promised. The atmosphere was one of genuine love and happiness, with each and every person knowing just how far God's protection and love had extended to them that Christmas.

The kids made clear that they considered the holiday theirs, and after their simple play about the shepherds seeking the Christ Child, they lined up to receive candy from the Smiths. Soon the entire affair burst into a full-fledged party, with sweets and goodies spread out on a lace tablecloth. Someone brought out a punch bowl and cups, and soon everyone was toasting the day and the man who they hoped would stay to become one of Deer Ridge's own.

Finally, Tyler led them in a closing prayer. "Father, we thank You for the gift of Your Son. We can't begin to understand the sacrifice You made on our behalf, but we praise You for Your love."

Several people murmured in agreement before Tyler could continue, "You've watched over this town in a most wondrous way this day—and in a very unique and special way You brought us all together. For a while, we forgot our differences and divisions. For a very precious time, we were able to stand here before You, knowing with surety that Your gift was given equally to us all. In that gift we are given hope, forgiveness and eternal life. Thank You, Father. Amen."

There were few dry eyes in the room when Tyler finished. Beyond a murmured thank you or pat on the back, no one said a word to the young pastor as he left the school. They all knew where his heart was hurrying him.

seventeen

Amy restlessly pushed back her covers and started to sit up. She'd been in bed four days now; because of her mother's continual care, she was very nearly herself again. In spite of this, however, no one seemed inclined to let her out of bed.

"Oh, no, you don't, young lady." Her mother came into the room with a tray of food.

"I can't just lie here eating all the time," Amy protested. "I'll get fat and lazy!"

"You could do with a little more meat on your bones," Dora laughed. "As for lazy, that will be the day pigs fly."

Amy giggled and sat back reluctantly against the pillows. "I truly feel fine, Ma."

"I know." Dora put the tray across her daughter's lap. "You just let me pamper you a bit more. Soon enough, if I have that young preacher of yours figured out, you'll be gone from this house and my care—so let me enjoy it while I can."

Amy frowned slightly. Since the day after her rescue, she had not seen Tyler at all. She'd asked her father about him yesterday, but Charles had shrugged his shoulders. Perhaps Tyler needed to tend to business, he told her.

"You can just wipe that frown off your face," Dora commanded good-naturedly. "Tyler will be back."

"I hope so." Amy's voice lacked confidence. She glanced down at the tray on her lap; it held a bowl of beef stew, two biscuits, and a glass of milk. "Didn't I just eat an hour ago?" she asked with a laugh.

"Just be quiet and eat." Dora tucked the covers around her daughter. "I used Cora Peterson's recipe for the stew. I seem to recall that was your favorite."

Amy took a mouthful of the thick stew and nodded. "Mmm, it's perfect."

Dora smiled at this announcement and turned to leave. "Now, if you need anything at all, just ring." She nodded at the bell by Amy's bedside.

"I promise." Amy tried to give the stew her attention. When her mother had left the room, though, Amy sighed and pushed the tray back.

"Where are you, Tyler?" she whispered into the silent air. She didn't want to eat or rest anymore. She wanted to talk to Tyler. She needed to hear his voice and know that everything was truly all right.

Boredom was her enemy, and Amy wanted nothing more than to be up and about. At least if she were back to her regular duties, Tyler's absence wouldn't be so noticeable.

After ten or fifteen minutes, her mother reappeared. She gave the tray a glance and frowned. "You haven't eaten much of it." She looked at Amy for a long moment, and then she surprised her daughter by going to the closet and pulling out a long flannel robe. "Here." She handed Amy the robe and took the tray. "Put this on and I'll let you sit at the window."

Amy's smile stretched nearly from ear to ear. This was the first time her mother had agreed to let her get up for any reason other than the absolute necessities. Hurriedly, in case her mother changed her mind, she thrust her arms through the robe's sleeves.

Dora put the tray on the table by the window. "Now, seeing as how I'm being so nice to you, oblige me by eating a little more of this." She went back to help Amy to her feet. "You promise to just sit here, now?" Dora settled Amy in the chair. "No big ideas about trying to get up on your feet?"

"Of course not." Amy smiled.

Dora sniffed and looked at her daughter suspiciously. "You just mind what your mother says, girl." Her voice was stern, but the corners of her mouth curved up.

A knock at the bedroom door made them both turn. Charles peeked his head inside with a grin. "I found someone wandering around the yard below, hoping to get a chance to talk with our Amy," he teased. Pushing the door open wide, he revealed a grinning Tyler Andrews.

"Tyler!" Amy jumped to her feet.

"Sit back down!" Dora commanded. "You promised."

Amy obediently did as she was told, but a slight pout on her lips told them all that she wasn't happy about it.

"Now, if you promise," her mother stressed the words, "to stay put, we'll let Tyler visit you for a spell."

Amy nodded and made the sign of an "X" over her heart. "Cross my heart," she said solemnly.

Her parents and Tyler laughed. "I guess that's the best we can hope for," Charles said. "I'll get you a chair, Tyler," he added. "Be right back."

Dora smiled and exited the room quietly. Meanwhile, Amy tried to keep herself from leaping across the room into Tyler's arms.

"You shaved," she said with a grin.

"I was told it was quite overdue." Tyler returned her grin.

Charles entered the room with a kitchen chair, then just as quickly left. Tyler brought the chair to the table where Amy's food still sat untouched.

"You'd best eat that." He pointed to the stew.

"I'm not hungry," Amy said softly.

Tyler frowned. "You're still not feeling well?"

Amy made a face. "I feel fine. But Ma's been feeding me every five minutes—or so it seems. All I've really wanted to do was get up and. . ." She stopped abruptly and looked deep into Tyler's warm gaze.

"And?" Tyler prompted.

"And talk to you," she admitted. "Where have you been? I was beginning to get worried that I'd have to saddle up and come looking for you."

Tyler reached out and took hold of Amy's hand. He looked down at her fingers and then gave them a squeeze. "I'll never be far from you. I promise."

Amy felt warmth spread from her hand, up her arm, until it finally engulfed her whole body, leaving her trembling. "I've missed you," she whispered. "I never even had a chance to thank you for all that you did. Pa told me you were the one who figured things out. He told me that without your devotion to the search, I'd most likely have died."

Tyler said nothing. He knew the words were true, but they seemed unimportant just now. "I had to find you," he whispered.

"Yes," Amy said. A hint of amusement played at the corners of her mouth, but she made her voice carefully serious. "Mrs. Smith told me that she accidently told you about your Christmas gift. I suppose it was necessary to find me in order to be sure you got it."

Tyler looked surprised at her words, almost taken back for a moment, and Amy laughed. "Don't be so serious, Tyler. I was teasing."

Tyler shook his head and smiled sheepishly. "I guess

it's going to take me a while to get used to the idea that you're really here with me safe and sound—and even a little obnoxious. I was so afraid I'd lost you."

Amy smiled, but her eyes misted at the expression she saw on his face. "But I'm all right now, thanks to you and Pa and everyone else. God watched over me. Even when I gave up hope, He stood fast and provided for my rescue. I won't spend the rest of my life having you look at me that way." Her voice was firm.

Tyler pulled his hand away. "Look at you what way?"

"Like I'm about to disappear into thin air. Or," she lowered her voice to a whisper, "die."

Tyler considered her words for a moment. "I know you're right. I have to learn to trust your safety to God. But you did disappear into thin air—and you came awfully close to dying. Gallagher would have left you there in that soddy if we hadn't interfered. I don't think you could have survived much longer." He shook his head, his eyes dark.

"I know." Amy reached to take back Tyler's hand. "After what happened to your wife, I can understand how you must feel. But we are all in God's hands. And you must let go of your worry. I want to get on with my life. I want to make plans."

Tyler's face relaxed, and after a moment his mouth curved into a smile. "What? Beyond today?" he teased.

"Yes." She looked up at him. "You were right. It's easy to take one day at time when you have no one to plan for a future with. Now that I have you, I find my head just bursting with plans. But I don't think it can be all bad to make plans. Even Proverbs says that we can make our plans, counting on God to direct our path. I'll still try to live one day at a time. I don't want to miss even one of the wonderful blessings God has given me in the here and now. But while I'm doing that, I'm also going to look forward to the days to come. Just so long as our plans for the future are grounded in God's Word."

"Then maybe you'll need this." Tyler pulled his well-worn Bible from his coat pocket. He handed the book to Amy and watched as she gently ran her fingers across the cover. "Merry Christmas."

"I don't know what to say." Amy looked up at him with tears in her eyes. "I can't take your Bible." She blinked the tears away and saw now the amusement in Tyler's eyes.

"Well, you're right," he said. "I won't be able to get along without that Bible very well. That's why I have a confession to make."

"Oh? And what might that be?" Amy's voice was suspicious.

"The Bible is just a part of your Christmas gift."

"And what might the rest of my gift be?" Amy leaned forward.

Tyler shrugged, then held out his arms. "Me. It's a package deal. To get the Bible, you have to take me too. We kind of go together."

"I see." Amy hugged the Bible to her.

"Will you marry me, Amy Carmichael?" Tyler's voice was serious now.

"Of course I will." Amy breathed out a heavy sigh. "I was beginning to wonder how I was going to propose to you, what with you taking so long to ask that particular question. All this talk about Bibles."

Tyler laughed and got to his feet. He started to pull Amy up into his arms, and then suddenly he stopped and pushed her back down. "I forgot. You promised your ma you'd sit."

Amy frowned, but Tyler quickly remedied the situation by pulling his chair close to hers. Leaning over, he pulled her against him with one hand and lifted her face with the other. "I love you, Amy." He lowered his mouth to hers, his lips both gentle and firm.

Amy melted against him. She felt her heart nearly burst with love. When he pulled his lips away at last, she opened her eyes slowly and met his amused stare.

"When?" she whispered.

"I beg your pardon?"

She narrowed her eyes at him, but his golden hair beckoned her fingers, and she reached up to push back a strand before she answered. "You know very well what I mean, Tyler Andrews." She pursed her lips primly. "When can we get married, Parson?"

Tyler grinned. "I'll have to check my schedule and see when I can fit you in. Pastoring is a mighty big responsibility, you know. It might be a spell before I can get back to these parts and. . ."

Amy jerked away from his arms. "Don't tease me, Tyler Andrews. If I have to, I'll hitch up the team and drive us to Hays myself." She sighed and then added firmly, "I've never been pushy about anything in my life—until now. But I'm beginning to think Angie may have been right all along. She sees a thing she wants and goes right after it. Well, now I intend to do the same."

Tyler's raucous laughter filled the air, bringing Charles and Dora to the doorway.

"What's going on?" Charles gave Tyler and Amy an amused look.

"Your daughter," Tyler said, still laughing, "is threatening to to hitch up the team and drive us to Hays so we can get married. I was just picturing the sight in my mind.

Barely off her death bed, clad in her nightgown, hair all wild and crazy behind her," he paused, and Amy turned crimson at his description, "and she's going to drive us to Hays."

"It's always the quiet ones who'll surprise you," Charles advised Tyler. With an arm around his wife, Charles added, "And I speak from experience."

Tyler laughed all the more at that, and even Dora couldn't help but join in. Soon, Amy gave up trying to be serious and chuckled in spite of herself. With Tyler Andrews for a husband, she had no doubt she would always have laughter in her house.

❧

From that moment on, Tyler and Amy spent many hours together planning and preparing for their wedding. Tyler shared with her his prayerful consideration of the town's offer to become the full-time pastor, and Amy rejoiced when he decided to accept the job. She'd happily follow him anywhere, she knew in her heart, but she loved Deer Ridge and her family, and she was glad to stay close to all that she cared about.

She soon learned that Tyler's absence during her recovery had included a trip to Hays, where he had managed to find another preacher who would not only take over Tyler's circuit, but also returned to Deer Ridge with him. With the other preacher officiating, the wedding was to take place on New Year's Day. Amy couldn't imagine a better way to start the new year.

When the day came at last, she stood proudly beside the huge man. The drawn, nervous look on his face almost made her giggle, but her own nerves weren't much more settled than Tyler's appeared to be. She listened carefully to the words spoken by the circuit rider, and then she repeated her vows. Without a doubt in her heart, she promised to love, honor, and obey this man she loved so much.

Tyler's voice was firm and grave as he repeated the same vows. When he took her hand and placed a small gold band on her finger, tears of joy and wonder slid down Amy's cheeks.

Then the ceremony was over. Tyler pulled her into his arms, kissing her in front of the entire community. With a loud voice, he declared to one and all that they were joined in God's sight and in love.

The community cheered heartily as the ceremony concluded. They congratulated the young couple until Amy thought her hand would be permanently numb from shaking the hands of so many people.

Charles and Dora came to greet their children, and Amy smiled radiantly when they called her Mrs. Andrews. Angie in her wedding finery, a new gown of blue taffeta which had come from Hays, danced rings around everyone. The entire community was convinced that she'd be the next to marry. The only question was which one of her many suitors Angie would finally settle on.

"We're mighty glad to see you up and around, Miss Amy," Jeremy Smith said when his turn came to congratulate the newlyweds. He turned then to Tyler and broke into a broad grin. "And we're mighty happy, Preacher, to know we'll get to hear your preaching every week and not just once a month."

Tyler pulled Amy close. She lifted her face to see the look of pride and joy in her husband's eyes. "Deer Ridge will be a good place to call home," he replied, looking down into Amy's face. "A right fine place to plan a future."

Amy smiled. "You mean a future beyond today?" she whispered.

The joke was lost on Jeremy, but Tyler smiled as he looked down at Amy and nodded. "You can count on it, Mrs. Andrews." He gave her a wink. "I'm planning on spending a good long time with you beyond today. A whole lifetime, in fact."

A Letter To Our Readers

Dear Reader:

In order that we might better contribute to your reading enjoyment, we would appreciate your taking a few minutes to respond to the following questions. When completed, please return to the following:

Rebecca Germany, Editor
Heartsong Presents
P.O. Box 719
Uhrichsville, Ohio 44683

1. Did you enjoy reading *Beyond Today*?
   ☐ Very much. I would like to see more books
     by this author!
   ☐ Moderately
     I would have enjoyed it more if _____

   _____

2. Are you a member of *Heartsong Presents*? Yes   No
   If no, where did you purchase this book? _____

   _____

3. What influenced your decision to purchase
   this book? (Check those that apply.)

   ☐ Cover   ☐ Back cover copy
   ☐ Title   ☐ Friends
   ☐ Publicity   ☐ Other _____

4. On a scale from 1 (poor) to 10 (superior), please rate the following elements.

___Heroine   ___Plot

___Hero   ___Inspirational theme

___Setting   ___Secondary characters

5. What settings would you like to see covered in *Heartsong Presents* books?

_____

_____

6. What are some inspirational themes you would like to see treated in future books?_____

_____

_____

7. Would you be interested in reading other *Heartsong Presents* titles?   ❏ Yes   ❏ No

8. Please circle your age range:
❏ Under 18   ❏ 18-24   ❏ 25-34
❏ 35-45   ❏ 46-55   ❏ Over 55

9. How many hours per week do you read? _____

Name _____

Occupation _____

Address _____

City _____ State _____ Zip _____

JoAnn A. Grote
Historical Trilogy

___*The Sure Promise*—Haunted by her own lonely childhood, Laurina Dalen is determined to provide a home for the Wells children. Matthew Strong is determined to meet the medical needs of the prairie dwellers. Laurina and Matthew belong to the praire. . .but first they must belong to each other. HP36 $2.95

___*The Unfolding Heart*—As Millicent and Adam's attraction for each other grows, Millicent realizes she could never make a good wife for a minister. And even if she could, how could she ever bring herself to live with him amid the crudeness and danger of the frontier? HP51 $2.95

___*Treasure of the Heart*—John Wells leaves his fiancée in Minnesota to go in search of the reason for his father's murder. Among the Black Hills of South Dakota he finds the answers he needs, as well as a rare treasure of the heart, Jewell Emerson. HP55 $2.95

···· Hearts ♥ ong ····

Any 12 *Heartsong Presents* titles for only $26.95 *

HISTORICAL ROMANCE IS CHEAPER BY THE DOZEN!

Buy any assortment of twelve *Heartsong Presents* titles and save 25% off of the already discounted price of $2.95 each!

*plus $1.00 shipping and handling per order and sales tax where applicable.

HEARTSONG PRESENTS TITLES AVAILABLE NOW:

__HP 1 A TORCH FOR TRINITY, *Colleen L. Reece*
__HP 2 WILDFLOWER HARVEST, *Colleen L. Reece*
__HP 3 RESTORE THE JOY, *Sara Mitchell*
__HP 4 REFLECTIONS OF THE HEART, *Sally Laity*
__HP 7 CANDLESHINE, *Colleen L. Reece*
__HP 8 DESERT ROSE, *Colleen L. Reece*
__HP11 RIVER OF FIRE, *Jacquelyn Cook*
__HP12 COTTONWOOD DREAMS, *Norene Morris*
__HP15 WHISPERS ON THE WIND, *Maryn Langer*
__HP16 SILENCE IN THE SAGE, *Colleen L. Reece*
__HP19 A PLACE TO BELONG, *Janelle Jamison*
__HP20 SHORES OF PROMISE, *Kate Blackwell*
__HP23 GONE WEST, *Kathleen Karr*
__HP24 WHISPERS IN THE WILDERNESS, *Colleen L. Reece*
__HP27 BEYOND THE SEARCHING RIVER, *Jacquelyn Cook*
__HP28 DAKOTA DAWN, *Lauraine Snelling*
__HP31 DREAM SPINNER, *Sally Laity*
__HP32 THE PROMISED LAND, *Kathleen Karr*
__HP35 WHEN COMES THE DAWN, *Brenda Bancroft*
__HP36 THE SURE PROMISE, *JoAnn A. Grote*
__HP39 RAINBOW HARVEST, *Norene Morris*
__HP40 PERFECT LOVE, *Janelle Jamison*
__HP43 VEILED JOY, *Colleen L. Reece*
__HP44 DAKOTA DREAM, *Lauraine Snelling*
__HP47 TENDER JOURNEYS, *Janelle Jamison*
__HP48 SHORES OF DELIVERANCE, *Kate Blackwell*

(If ordering from this page, please remember to include it with the order form.)

···· Presents ····

Great Inspirational Romance at a Great Price!

Heartsong Presents books are inspirational romances in contemporary and historical settings, designed to give you an enjoyable, spirit-lifting reading experience. You can choose from 88 wonderfully written titles from some of today's best authors like Colleen L. Reece, Brenda Bancroft, Janelle Jamison, and many others.

When ordering quantities less than twelve, above titles are $2.95 each.

SEND TO: Heartsong Presents Reader's Service
P.O. Box 719, Uhrichsville, Ohio 44683

Please send me the items checked above. I am enclosing $ _____
(please add $1.00 to cover postage per order. OH add 6.5% tax. PA and NJ add 6%.). Send check or money order, no cash or C.O.D.s, please.
To place a credit card order, call 1-800-847-8270.

NAME _____

ADDRESS _____

CITY/STATE_____ ZIP _____

LOVE A GREAT LOVE STORY?
Introducing Heartsong Presents —
Your Inspirational Book Club

Heartsong Presents Christian romance reader's service will provide you with four never before published romance titles every month! In fact, your books will be mailed to you at the same time advance copies are sent to book reviewers. You'll preview each of these new and unabridged books before they are released to the general public.

These books are filled with the kind of stories you have been longing for—stories of courtship, chivalry, honor, and virtue. Strong characters and riveting plot lines will make you want to read on and on. Romance is not dead, and each of these romantic tales will remind you that Christian faith is still the vital ingredient in an intimate relationship filled with true love and honest devotion.

Sign up today to receive your first set. Send no money now. We'll bill you only $9.97 post-paid with your shipment. Then every month you'll automatically receive the latest four "hot off the press" titles for the same low post-paid price of $9.97. That's a savings of 50% off the $4.95 cover price. When you consider the exaggerated shipping charges of other book clubs, your savings are even greater!

THERE IS NO RISK—you may cancel at any time without obligation. And if you aren't completely satisfied with any selection, return it for an immediate refund.

TO JOIN, just complete the coupon below, mail it today, and get ready for hours of wholesome entertainment.

Now you can curl up, relax, and enjoy some great reading full of the warmhearted spirit of romance.